THE NERVE

The 1998 Virago Book of Writing Women

edited by
Andrea Badenoch,
Maggie Hannan,
Pippa Little,
Debbie Taylor

A *Virago* book

Published by Virago Press 1998

This collection and introduction copyright © Andrea
Badenoch, Maggie Hannan, Pippa Little, Debbie Taylor.
Copyright © for each story held by the author.

Writing Women is supported by

Acknowledgements are due to the editors of the following publications
in which some of the poems first appeared: *Ambit*, *Blade*, *The Echo Room*,
Envoi, *Fatchance*, the *Forward Book of Poetry*, *The North*, *Poems on the*
Underground, *Poet's England*, *Purple Patch*, *The Rialto*, *Smiths Knoll*,
Writing Women. The story 'A kitten called Ursula' was
first published in *Staple* magazine.

A CIP catalogue record for this book is
available from the British Library

ISBN 1 86049 575 3

Typeset in Novarese by M Rules
Printed and bound in Great Britain by
Clays Ltd, St Ives plc

Virago
A Division of
Little, Brown and Company (UK)
Brettenham House
Lancaster Place
London WC2E 7EN

Contents

Contents

Poetry editors

MAGGIE HANNAN lives in Hull, where she studied Philosophy before becoming a poet. She has worked as a stonemason, professional life model and charlady to subsidise her writing. She won a Gregory Award in 1990 and her first collection *Liar, Jones* (Bloodaxe, 1992) was widely acclaimed. She was one of the first Writers in Residence on the Internet, where she launched the virtual magazine *Grim*.

PIPPA LITTLE lives in Northumbria and has three children and a doctorate in women's poetry. Her writing career began in print journalism in Scotland, where she won a Young Scots Poet award and a Gregory Award for her poetry. She now teaches creative writing and literature in Newcastle upon Tyne at the university and in adult education. Her poems have appeared in every major poetry journal.

Prose editors

ANDREA BADENOCH lives in Newcastle upon Tyne, has three children and an MA in American women writers. She worked in welfare rights in Bristol and London before returning north. She has run literature and women's studies courses to finance her writing and is author of *Women Like Us: Modern Fiction* (Virago, 1992) and the crime thriller *Mortal* (Macmillan, 1998).

DEBBIE TAYLOR lives in Newcastle upon Tyne, has one child and a PhD in Psychology. After two years living in a traditional African village, she returned to England to become editor of the award-winning *New Internationalist* magazine. Her fourth book of non-fiction (*My Children, My Gold*, Virago, 1994) was shortlisted for the Fawcett Prize for women's writing. Her second novel, *The Empress and the Dwarf* (Allison and Busby), will be published in 1999.

Introduction

'Have you ever eaten cocoa by the spoonful, straight from the tub? It is an art.' This is how the first piece in this anthology begins. Reading through the poems and stories collected here is an equally sensual – but slightly fraught – experience. 'It coats your teeth. You suck and swallow, pulling the dark flavours into your throat. There is none of the joy of chocolate, but some of the secrets. Bitter and unlikely.'

This volume is the first in what we hope will be an enduring partnership between Virago Press and *Writing Women* magazine. Each year the editors will contact every writing group, publication and course in the country looking for authors on the brink of their writing careers: women who have honed their craft and found their voice, but have not yet been discovered by a mainstream publisher. From over three thousand submissions this year, we have selected twelve poets and twelve prose writers whose work provides a challenging new perspective on what constitutes 'women's writing' at the end of the nineties.

You will find no feminist didactics here. Though many of the pieces are in the first person, there are no lurid confessionals or lesbian awakenings. On the contrary, use of the first person lends an edgy intimacy that allows for a subtle exploration of subjects at one remove from typical women's themes. The authors here may be writing as women, but this is not the usual women's subject matter.

The sensuality's still there, of course, the eating and loving that has always characterised women's writing. But there is a dangerous edge to many of these pieces: the elegant Mrs Beecham convulsing with secret pleasure at the hairdresser's; barefoot Camilla eating yoghurt with her fingers and making her lover drink blood; bald Eva whose eyebrows and palm-prints were seared off in a fire; Dr 0 serving vodka in a jagged bean tin. The poems contain equally sensual but disturbing images: the woman carrying a swan under her arm 'like a briefcase'; the boy who skins and stuffs his pet animals. *Bitter and unlikely*.

This sharper edge bears little resemblance to the brattishness some male writers excel in. The contents here may shock, but there is a tenderness and wit which redeem the work and leave you feeling delighted rather than disgusted.

Writing Women magazine has been publishing new work by women for nearly twenty years. Poets and novelists like Helen Dunmore, Linda France and Selima Hill had some of their first pieces printed in its pages. Based in Newcastle upon Tyne, its team of editors has been able to tap into a sophisticated and flourishing literary scene in the North of England, a scene which has proved particularly nurturing for woman writers.

Women's anthologies have become something of a cliché

these days. What began as a real need to give woman authors a space of their own – to counter the masculine bias in the sixties and seventies – has become one of the quiet publishing successes of the eighties and nineties. There is now a substantial loyal and discriminating market of women who specifically seek out and buy poetry and prose by other women. If there is a need now, it is not for more writing by established authors. It is for a publication that will give an insight into what's happening in women's literature: what's good, what's fashionable, what names to look out for in the future.

The biographical details at the end of the book reveal that the contributors are predominantly mature, and predominantly northern. Only one is in her twenties; only four live in London. By contrast, five of the authors (who produced some of the most modern and vibrant of the contributions) are in their fifties; and thirteen live in the North. This may come as something of a surprise to those who expect exciting new literature to be produced largely by young Londoners.

If nothing else, this collection proves that 'modern' does not necessarily mean 'young'. On the contrary, it takes time and perseverance to lose the didacticism, cliché and banal passion of the immature writer. Authors, like visual artists, must practise their craft before they can produce good work. The vast majority of the women in this book are committed authors who have been writing for years. Many teach creative writing themselves, or are studying it as mature students. Many run or belong to writers' groups. Others have abandoned lucrative careers to concentrate on their work.

Their dedication shows in the sheer standard of the writing. The poems are all carefully and cleverly crafted; the prose is sharp, tight and sophisticated. The fresh exuberance of many of the pieces stems not from the slapdash rawness of the beginner, but from the subtlety and skill of the mature author.

'Black lines, like dried blood, trace the shape of your lips. Your teeth, if they are brown, look rotten and hungry. You savour the final flecks of flavour as you wipe your mouth.

'Then you are ready to smile.'

Andrea Badenoch, Maggie Hannan,
Pippa Little, Debbie Taylor

For details of how to submit to the next anthology, please send a sae to Writing Women, PO Box 111, Newcastle-upon-Tyne NE3 1WF.

THE NERVE

HARRIET KLINE

Red herrings

Have you ever eaten cocoa by the spoonful, straight from the tub? It is an art. An operation more delicate than removing a splinter. It requires a steady hand, a muscular mouth, an ability to hold and control your breath. Cocoa is as fine as fairy dust. Inhale at the wrong time and you'll cough the whole lot down your favourite shirt. Trampish stains. Evidence of undignified behaviour.

So you must not pile the spoon too high. You have to clamp your mouth around it, slide it out through tight lips. The cocoa is a wet lump clinging to the roof of your mouth. But there are pockets of wispy, dry powder; they can choke you still.

You rub your tongue around your mouth and the cocoa grows heavy. It coats your teeth. You suck and swallow, pulling the dark flavours into your throat. There is none of the joy of chocolate, but some of the secrets. Bitter and unlikely.

Last of all, you have to rinse your mouth out thoroughly.

Black lines, like dried blood, trace the shape of your lips. Your teeth, if they are brown, look rotten and hungry. You savour the final flecks of flavour as you wipe your mouth.

Then you are ready to smile.

My brother is making chocolate sauce. No cocoa for him. It is too cheap and reminds him of cardigans and old-men's pantries. He melts finest Swiss chocolate in a bowl and I breathe the sweetness in the kitchen. My mouth is wide. I would like to swallow the air. There are dark splinters of chocolate on the white plate. I would pick them up with moistened fingers, but I know that Chris will snarl. He is the cook today.

He is creating a meal to impress. A meal that will make a woman love him. I must not destroy it with my grubby fingers, my greedy thoughts. He has drawn a line across the kitchen floor. I may not cross it except at his bidding. When there are pans to scrub, napkins to fold into delicate crowns, he will invite me over. But not when his food is exposed. He thinks I'll drool.

His spoon, glistening with melted chocolate moves from bowl to bowl. My eyes follow, like a cat at a fish tank. My hand even twitches, like a cat's paw uselessly patting the glass. But I can restrain myself. My mouth is warm, flooded, but I swallow. Chris is cruel. When he has finished with the chocolate bowl he looks over and smiles. I step forward. He holds the bowl aloft for one beautiful moment, then plunges it into greasy, grey dishwater.

Have you ever lost your pudding before it's finished? It is a trauma. I lost a treacle tart and custard once. I'd had five sweet mouthfuls before the phone rang. I ran to it, spoke, laughed, listened, all with half my mind on the treacle tart. But when the call was over, it was nowhere to be found.

I was distraught. I looked in ridiculous places. Under the bed, behind the sofa cushions, even out in the garden. Twice.

Chris shrugged. 'You must have eaten it all.' He was bored with the sound of my voice. I must have said pudding a hundred times.

But I knew it was not finished. The last mouthful of a pudding is the most important. You have to savour it, then shut your mind away from the taste. If you don't, you'll just go back for second, third helpings until your ribs ache from the pressure of the food. You have to tell yourself it's over.

This had not happened with my treacle tart. I could not picture the film of custard in the empty bowl, the tracks made by my scraping spoon. I stamped my foot, drove Chris out of the flat with my rage.

I found the pudding later, on a high shelf. But I was too miserable to enjoy it. The pleasures of treacle tart are soft ones and my body was stiff and angry. I forced the tart down, went back for seconds.

Chris has redrawn the line across the kitchen and I am even further from the chopping board. He is making tortellini. Special ones, a single egg yolk in each pasta case. They will be dunked in boiling water, at the very last minute. The pasta cooks, the yolk remains liquid. A golden sauce to swirl around asparagus tips and fine green beans.

'This requires extreme delicacy,' he says, for the third time. One greedy lunge from me and the whole lot is ruined. Not just his dinner party but his love life too. Lillian will hardly be enthralled by a lump of sticky orange dough, reeking of boiled eggs. Of course I have no intention of lunging, or drooling, or ruining his chance of love, but he checks my every movement with hard, suspicious eyes.

I have promised not to enthuse too much at the table. Last week when I made apple pie, I loved each mouthful. Chris claims that I groaned over every single one. He said he was embarrassed, but did not stop me because it was my dinner party and I could do as I pleased. But tonight he is in charge. I can say 'mmmm' discreetly if I must, but only once, for each course.

'How about once for each different foodstuff?' I ask. 'It's stupid only saying "mmmm" when I taste the tortellini. Supposing I like the asparagus better?'

But Chris is firm. No fuss. He wants to pretend we always eat like this. That's why I have to wash up before the meal. Any evidence of effort must be hidden from Lillian. No flour caked to the surfaces, no pools of starch glistening on the hob. The table set and the napkins folded.

How different from my dinner parties. Last week I made salads in big bowls and five different dips. We sat on the floor, leaned across each other, spooning beautiful colours on to tortilla. We held the rolls of pastry high. Sauces dribbled on to our wrists and we sucked our fingers noisily. Chris loved it, tried out all possible combinations, stained his jeans with blood red salsa. But tonight we must be genteel. We will bend our wrists over shining cutlery. Sip wine, refrain from poking the candles to make the wax dribble down.

I decide to invite Lillian, whoever she is, to my next party. Show her what he's really like. Chris, unaware of my plans, presses his fingers around the last tortellini. He places the whole plateful on a high shelf, out of my reach.

*

Have you ever risen in the night and longed for beef tea? It is very frustrating. I am a vegetarian and have never tasted beef tea, but I imagine it salty and rich, more comforting than Horlicks. When the wind howls in the middle of the night I wish I had a granny. The sort who would sit in a rocker by the hearth, cat on her knee. There would be a black pot, constantly simmering over the embers beside her. Bones, offal, bay leaf, every scrap of food saved and boiled up into dark, beef tea. I'd sit at her feet with a blanket over my toes, hold my cup with both hands. The steam would wet my cheeks, grease would coat my mouth.

Some nights I've pulled on my dressing gown, boiled the kettle and brewed up the most hideous concoctions. Marmite, peanut butter, a dash of paprika, a pinch of mixed herbs. Disgusting. I spit them into the sink, rinse the mug repeatedly in the morning. Do you think there's anyone in England, now, who drinks real beef tea?

Cocoa, lost puddings and beef tea make good conversations at dinner parties. People laugh. Their bellies are full so their laughter lodges, almost painfully, in their necks. But this afternoon, as we empty the bin, Chris shakes his finger at me. I am forbidden to mention anything of the sort tonight. I lug the big bag down the stairs and Chris holds the doors open, glaring.

'You're obsessed with food,' he says. 'You and all women. It's not as funny as you think. It's just embarrassing.'

I stop at the rubbish chute and throw the bag down at my feet.

'Well, how strange,' I say, hands on hips. 'I remember Louise and Lisa laughing uncontrollably at my party last week.' This is true. Louise shed silent tears, smudging her mascara. Lisa's laugh surprised me. So sonorous for one so small. It was the first sound she'd made all evening. Chris turns away from me, picks the flaking paint on the balcony rails.

'Yeah, but we weren't all amused, you know,' he mutters down into his jumper. 'John and Olly weren't exactly rolling round in hysterics.' I hoist the rubbish up to the mouth of the chute, and try to remember Olly and John at my party. I didn't take much notice of them at the time, I was laughing too much. Louise confessed that she used to drink whole tins of evaporated milk and I loved her for it. But I could remember them now. They exchanged glances. Eyes raised to the ceiling, long-suffering boredom.

I push the rubbish into the chute. We hear it slide down, thump at the bottom. I think about boring dinner parties. Men talking, not listening to each other. Women yawning into wine-glasses, pointing their pleasant, but motionless faces at each man who speaks. Mouths clamped shut, thoughts on shopping lists, sex or escape. They don't make a show of their boredom, unlike Chris and his friends.

I make the mistake of saying this. I tell him that beef tea and puddings give women a look in for once. He marches towards me, his face flushed with anger.

'You're going to ruin my party. I can tell. You and your feminism.'

Foul smells rise from the mouth of the rubbish chute. We both wince and step away. Mouldering rubbish from split bags has been disturbed. I am ready to laugh at this, but Chris turns and slams through the double door. I hear his feet echo up the stairs. I do not follow him. I go to the balcony rail, try to breathe deeply, calm down.

We cannot see the sea from here. We are not high enough. We see the opposite block, their identical windows, their rubbish chute, their oval of perfect green grass at the bottom. But we can smell it. I have never noticed this before, but now my big angry breaths are drawing in gulps of sea air. I smell salt and sand, and boats. I smell long walks with the sound of the waves and gulls. I smell shells and sand between my toes. I have been on this balcony countless times and never noticed this gift in the wind. Now I will always pause and draw it in, two streams of pleasure through my nostrils.

I return to the flat, revived, but Chris speaks before I can smile.

'How am I supposed to impress Lillian now? You've put me in a temper.' He paces the living room. 'If you don't promise not to ask those questions, you're not invited any more.'

I remain calm. 'Chris, I promise. Now go for a long walk on the beach. Clear your head. Don't come back till seven. You'll have plenty of time to dress and shave before anyone arrives.' I fetch his coat and hold it out for him. His face relaxes and he leaves, pattering down the stairs.

I stretch my arms up high. I open the windows wide, breathe in the air, enjoy with every sinew the silence in the flat. I am not obsessed by food, I think, I am obsessed by life.

Have you ever taken a longer route home just so you could smell a lilac bush? It's always worth it. There's one outside the probation office, just a few streets from here. Even with heavy shopping bags, I walk that way. It only takes five more minutes. And it is wonderful just to stop. Lean forward, breathe deeply, let the smell curl into your body. It is a sweet smell, sharp and magical.

It magics up memories. With my head in the lilacs, I see my mother's hall. A vase of flowers reflected deep in polished wood. A scattering of tiny petals. Cool air, the hat stand, the sombre tick of the grandfather clock. Other times I see my friend's garden. The dappled light, the cat blinking, the clink of the trowel against a buried stone. Or I see old ladies in perfume and pearls, or garlands at a May Day dance. A new picture every time. This magic helps me with my heavy bags. Helps me through the day.

In spite of everything, I love Chris. So I hoover the flat. I polish the wineglasses, fold the napkins, scrub the cooker, and only once dip my finger in the chocolate sauce. Then I lie down exhausted. When the phone rings I close my eyes. I leave it to the answering machine.

'Hi Chris, It's Lillian here.' She has a soft voice, like a mother singing a lullaby. My eyes snap open. 'I'm so sorry, I forgot to say I'm allergic to eggs. Hope you weren't planning on making omelette tonight.' She gives a little laugh. So she knows that Chris disdains such simple fare. 'Hope this won't cause you too much hassle. I'll see you later. Bye.'

My rest is over. I grab my coat, run out on to the stairs. But I stop halfway down. I don't know which way Chris has gone. The beach is long. No point in me charging along the front, waving my arms. I return to the flat. I have an hour and a half. I have to make something spectacular. Something to impress, but which won't make too much washing up. The flat must stay spotless.

I pace and think. I open the fridge. Four Marks and Spencer onion bhajis. I could pretend Chris made them. But he wouldn't want Lillian to think he was a curry freak. He likes sophisticated food. Two pounds of strong Cheddar, a pot of yoghurt, half a tin of plum tomatoes. My herrings. Six of them. They were to be for lunch tomorrow. Delicious grilled with a pinch of paprika. But a bit simple. If we are going to pretend that Chris made the dinner we don't want her to think he made no effort at all.

I pace and think. It will have to be herring. Fish is fashionable, at least. They just need to be made spectacular. A coating. Something clever and saucy. I want to run to the window, yell for Chris into the wind. I am angry that he is not here. If he didn't have such a temper, he could invent some brilliant dish to delight her. I could be asleep. But no, I am picking up the pieces. Reliable sister sorts everything out. My anger takes hold again. I think of his stupid accusations at the rubbish chute. I walk faster and faster. The sun is setting. The cutlery, laid out neatly, glints and glows orange. Inspiration strikes me. I'll show him, I think. He can't go round saying I'm obsessed by food. Yes, I'll show him.

Have you ever left a room and then rushed back for a view of the sunset? I can hardly help myself. I'm compelled to stop, and look right into the sky, press my hands against the window pane. Even when I'm hurrying, I'll stop for just a second.

It's not as if sunsets are a novelty. I've seen every kind. Violent frowning ones with black clouds and fiery tongues. Demure ones blushing at a single early star. Brocaded clouds or silent empty skies, I grab them all with my eyes. I daren't miss a moment.

I think I'm afraid of missing out. I don't want to be the child who missed the party. Who didn't see the bully fall in the pond, who can't say 'It was the time of my life'. So I drink in the sunset.

I witness the beauty as if it will somehow make me special and beautiful for noticing it. I have taken part fully in life.

Chris's face is ashen when he returns. He has smelled the cooking on the stairs, heard the clang of the pans. Anger makes him rigid. His shoulders hoisted up to his ears. I stir the pan and point to the answering machine. The sauce is deep red. Bursting bubbles flick tiny specks on to the white stove. Lillian's voice is calm but Chris leaps into the air. Now he is as red as the sauce. He runs to his coat, grabs car keys, squints at the clock then throws his coat back down. Next he runs to the fridge, retreats, flops on to the sofa. Defeated.

'It's all right, Chris,' I say. I imitate Lillian's lullaby voice. 'We're having herring, in a complicated sauce. If it goes down well, you just whisked it up in five minutes.' He looks at me sceptically as I add another pinch of ginger. 'And if it doesn't work, then I made dinner. You were called out on urgent business.'

He sits back and grins. But doesn't thank me. He doesn't notice the spotless room, the cut flowers on the mantelpiece. So I slurp noisily at the wooden spoon until he looks suitably annoyed. The absence of a reprimand will do in place of thanks. I point to the blender.

'You'd better wash that up, Chris, so there's no clutter.' He is almost meek as he obeys. I want to poke him in the ribs with the wooden spoon. Stain his shirt with tomato and Tabasco.

Do you know that feeling, early in spring, when it is suddenly warm enough to wear a skirt without tights? Oh, it is wonderful. Soft fabric swishes over my skin. My thighs brush together. I am aware of every step. The air beneath my skirt is my secret. My thighs are my secret. I walk with a smile, and the world warms me. One of my favourite feelings of the year.

'Mmmm, me too!' Lillian looks up from her plate. The back-bone of her herring hangs like a millipede from her fork. She has lifted it easily from the flesh. No bones left behind to choke on. 'It's almost sexy, isn't it?' she continues, and flashes a quick, blushing look at Chris. He quivers. He wants to glare at me for asking outrageous questions. But he wants to look knowingly at Lillian too. She lays her millipede delicately on to the spare plate and smiles wider.

'Amazing fish this,' she continues. 'Never tasted anything like it.'

'Chris is a brilliant cook,' I say quickly. 'Speciality is food from Tuscany.' Lillian smiles even wider.

'I'll have to come again, then. I love Italian food. Well, all food, actually.'

'Me too.' I look innocently at Chris. 'In fact I'm obsessed with food. And wearing skirts without tights. And sunsets and smells and birdsong.'

Lillian nods emphatically. 'And sex,' she says. 'It's all the same thing. If you love food, you love everything else. The sensual world.'

Now I dare not look at Chris. But he has acquired a lover, that much is clear. Thanks to me, of course, his reliable sister. He had better be grateful. There had better be second helpings of pudding for me. Lillian wipes the last sauce from her plate with her finger, leaving a white swath of china behind. Chris doesn't seem to mind. He has moved his chair a little closer to hers.

'So what is this dish called, then? Where is it from?' she asks him.

'I'm not sure, er, I can't remember. Known it for years.' His voice is faint, he is blushing. I step in quickly.

'Oh, this is what's known as a red herring.' I disturb an intimate look between them. But I continue. 'Quite an interesting story actually. It's based on some obscure belief about pleasure. That it is embarrassing. That to express enjoyment is obsession.' Chris's face is pale once more and his lips set in a thin line. Luckily, Lillian's eyes are on me. I fortify myself with a gulp of wine. 'Herring were scarce once, you see, and prized highly. But it was etiquette to pretend you ate them every day. Serve them casually, no excitement allowed. Anyone who betrayed their pleasure, with an untoward flick of the lips, a little blush, they were expelled from the table. Cast out as embarrassing. It began to affect other aspects of the society. People stopped showing any pleasure at all. Beautiful dresses were said to be old rags, thrown on at the last minute. Houses with glorious vistas kept their shutters closed. They were afraid of being called herring eaters if they gazed at the view too long. To say "I love you" was virtually a crime.

'But luckily the sister of the king had plenty of sense. She invented this sauce. She knew it was delicious and had it taken out on to the streets. Splashed heartily on to the plates in every house where herring were eaten. She knew this would reverse the trend. And it did. From that day on, it was law that herring must always be eaten with relish.'

Chris swallows. His hand shakes as he reaches for his glass. Lillian regards me doubtfully. Then, quite suddenly her face is bright with laughter. It rings out across the room. I grin. She laughs so hard that she has to rest her head on Chris's shoulder. He strokes her hair. Mission accomplished.

'Have you ever eaten cocoa straight from the jar?' I ask. Chris does not flinch.

LIZ ATKIN

It is as if Giacometti's dog

is alive and living in leafy
Hexham with an elderly woman –

a pure white whippet he is blade
thin, skeletal armature for Dog,
tiny biscuit-barrel of ribs
atop pipe-cleaner legs
tail wire curled under.

Too sharp to stroke
his eyes and nose are all
that seem alive, his bleached bark
a hollowed-out howl of wind –

he clicks quiet and stiff
behind her round the house,
but with her eyesight nearly gone
she thinks him dead
and only sees his ghost.

The ballroom fossil

Palaeontologists in years to come
might find this more interesting
than the commonplace names
paired for each other
and single lumpen imprints
embedded in grey concrete.

For these impressions
of petrified poise
suggest a four-legged beast
with hard and soft side
and a two-heart tempo
of 48 bar beats per minute
executing quickstep quarter-turns
with temporary elegance –

but they'll never flesh out
these footprint fossils
following a Victor Silvester diagram
to learn more of the creature
that turned time back
in anticlockwise circles
twice a week for years.

Head transplants

It was hidden amongst
the Weddings and Diamond Teas
in the rusting Peek Frean tin,
a ten by eight shock
of my late grandparents
familiar smiling heads
transplanted atop two aged
stark naked bodies –

his body sagged rickety astride
the wattled sac and flopped neck
of a decapitated turkey,
hers was propped alongside
nipples hanging like loose buttons,
one hand a broken fan
on an unironed abdomen.

They stood on sand and pine needles,
a high corrugated iron fence
with sea-blue horizon
painted on its undulations –
I wanted to be young enough again
to take some fat wax crayons
and quickly colour their ghosts in
staying within the lines.

The enterprise scheme

Pet heaven ends in the allotment shed
where they're measured muzzle to tail-tip
before the incision with a cobbler's knife
when guts with eyes go over the neighbours' roses.

After the faint bark of the head saw
fingers talcumed with home-made preservative
fumble plugs and bungs,
never much good at Art he misshapes
wire armatures of artificial body to wear
skin stuffed with lumpen wooden wool,
a surgical sliver then embroiders
slits lips and anal orifice.

From stiff-legged dogs to budgies
he breaks bones for a grin
and wings for a perch pinned
'attitude of flight' – for that human look
his secret lies in cheap dolls' eyes.
Now they await collection in frolic
contortions, pet hell beginning
as you see their own discarded bones
hammered between bloodied jaws.

Camilla's gift

For nights on end she forced me to have orgasms I didn't want. I would wake to the blind rhythm of mechanical stimulation. There were never any tender preliminaries.

'Why are you doing this when you know that sleep is all I want?' I asked her. 'Why are you so bloody spiteful?'

'It's the voices,' she replied. 'I have to obey them otherwise I'll be punished. When you get better I can stop.'

I succumbed with no pretence at pleasure, occasionally climaxing with a brief shudder that didn't placate her.

'Is that all?'

'It'll have to do, for Christ's sake. I'm a sick woman. What more do you want?'

'I want you to get better,' she said with all the stubborn helplessness of a small child.

I had long given up all hope of recovery and said nothing.

In the early days we would lie together for hours, gently

caressing. She loved the way I fucked her and didn't mind that I was always in control. Later she began to show signs of resentment by getting rough. She would tantalise but not let me touch her, and when the voices came the tables turned completely.

Late one night after the usual torture, she danced about the flat singing at the top of her voice. Every light blazed while she looked for something to eat. I could hear her banging about in the kitchen before she came back to bed with half a loaf of bread and a carton of yoghurt. Crumbling the bread into the yoghurt to make a thick lumpy paste, she ate with her fingers. She stuck her tongue directly into the carton to get to the last of the yoghurt and licked her hands clean. When she had done with licking herself, we were allowed to sleep. She snuggled up to my breasts and asked: 'How do you feel?'

'The same.'

'I care for you very much, I do really.'

'I'm glad to hear it.'

'But if you don't get better soon, I'll have to kill you.'

The spring before she came was the coldest on record for half a century: hardly a spring really, more of a flattening out of winter, a lengthening of the daylight hours in which to observe the gloom. There had been blizzards the previous November, then everything was frozen solid until April. I watched the muffled world from my window, saw the snow dissolve around the lake, the grass underneath still brown from last year's heatwave. In May frost attacked the new leaves.

I counted the days and thought: The weather is spiteful. It likes to upset people just for the hell of it. I think differently now. I think the weather likes to tease and it's we who have no

sense of humour. When I was at my sickest I thought the unsea-
sonal cold was my fault for overstaying my welcome. I thought
if only I could die, summer would come, but I kept opening my
eyes on another accusing day and a window stained with
pigeon shit.

June crept in under clouds more like concrete than vapour
for the amount of sunlight filtering through. Ducks fought seagulls for food on the island in the lake. There were no fledglings
in sight. Life, suspended and curled in on itself, waited for
something better.

My visitors chatted about the low water table and the
drought with forced cheerfulness. There would be a hosepipe
ban they said earnestly: as if I had a garden to fret over, as if I
cared! I observed their movements in detail and thought how
curious to belong to such an ugly species. What unnatural-
looking creatures we humans are! I smiled dutifully, waiting for
them to go. I'd already given up watching television and listening to the radio. It upset me then and still does now. I prefer
silence.

Unable to stand another minute of the freezing summer, my
home-help and district nurse went south for their holidays.
How would I manage, they wanted to know. They looked at me
with concern, guilt even.

'The neighbours will do my shopping. My friends will stop
by. Go, enjoy yourselves,' I told them. 'Don't worry about me.
I'll be fine.' They looked relieved.

It started to rain, a slow steady dripping which carried on
monotonously. At least it washed the dirt from my window. I
occupied myself counting droplets hitting the surface of the
lake. Buildings shimmered across the water. The reflection of
traffic lights on the wet roads became a source of fascination as

they shifted from red to green and back again. On my side of the lake the café-bars with their outdoor tables stood deserted. Normally Copenhagen buzzes with tourists in the summer: southerners in search of northern light and unspoilt beaches flock here to get ripped off. But this year they stayed sensibly at home. I listened with amusement to people coughing on the stairs outside my front door and thought: Good, why should I be the only one to suffer?

One Sunday night the sky pitched out hail, lightning, thunder and driving rain. It was already late when I heard frantic hammering at my door. Shit, someone must have forgotten to close the street door. I tried to ignore the persistent banging.

'Who is it?' Keeping the door on the safety chain, I opened it a crack.

'Please let me in. I've got nowhere to go.'

The drenched person out there looked little more than a child, so I let her in. She was so wet, a puddle formed where she stood. Ushering her into the bathroom, I offered towels and my own bathrobe. Soon she was nursing a mug of coffee and gratefully munching the biscuits I put in front of her. She smiled at me and what I'd thought was a spot of decay on one of her front teeth, turned out to be a diamond set in a small gold bezel.

'What's your name?'

'Camilla. I know there're lots of women called Camilla, but not all of them are me.'

I thought about this briefly. 'Surely none of the others are you?'

'No. Not all of them are me. You don't understand.'

Obviously not, but I changed the subject. 'I'm Laura.' (I'd never given my connection to other Lauras a moment's thought.)

'You look very old. How old are you?'

'Old enough. How old are you?'

She looked at her hands, apparently counting on her fingers. 'I'm not sure. Twenty, I think. What kind of cripple are you?'

'I'm dying of cancer.'

'Is it because you've done lots of bad things?'

'I haven't done bad things. At least I don't think so.'

'Then why are you dying?'

'That's not a question I can answer.'

Her eyes filled with tears. 'I don't want you to die. I think you're a nice person.'

I found myself becoming efficient and parental. 'Don't worry about it. People die all the time. If you've got nowhere to go, you'd better spend the night here and we can sort you out in the morning.' I gathered our mugs, hauled a spare duvet and pillow out of the linen cupboard. 'You'll find the sofa quite comfortable, and make yourself another hot drink if you want. But you must excuse me now, I need to sleep.'

I retired to my bedroom, but soon heard a soft scratching at the door.

'Yes, what is it?'

'I want to do something for you. Let me rub your feet. I'm good at it. It'll make you feel better.'

I'd already tucked myself in with a hot-water bottle, but I motioned for her to go ahead. Gently she slid a hand under the duvet and kneaded my icy foot.

'Why are you so cold?'

'Poor circulation!'

She *was* good and I grunted contentedly, observing how badly her hair had been cut. Blonde tufts stuck out at random, as if she'd been hacking away with nail scissors.

'Thank you, that was lovely. But we must stop now because I'm very tired.'

She looked disappointed. 'I've only done one foot. It doesn't matter if you fall asleep, let me do the other one.'

'This is as much as I can take. Honestly, I've hardly any energy.' I smiled at her reassuringly. 'Maybe tomorrow. I want to be alone now. Goodnight.'

She left quietly and I plummeted into a sleep more sound than I'd enjoyed for months. When I woke up in the morning, I found her curled up on the floor at the foot of my bed, without the duvet or pillow.

'What are you doing? You'll catch a terrible cold.'

'I'm guarding you from death. It's OK,' she grinned. 'I'm used to sleeping on the floor.'

'No need to be so dramatic!' I rose with the awareness that it had stopped raining and drew the blinds. Sunlight poured into the room. Beyond the window glistening foliage caught my eye.

'Isn't that beautiful!' She pulled the window open.

I couldn't stay irritable with her. Besides, I felt a lightness in my body I would not have believed was possible. I sent her to buy freshly baked rolls, while I ground coffee beans. The aroma was tantalising. I couldn't remember when last I'd looked forward to my breakfast so much. Hauling butter and cheese out of the fridge, I opened a new jar of marmalade. She returned with rolls, having picked flowers from window-boxes along the way. We put them in a tumblerful of water and ate in front of the open window. After breakfast she made herself useful around the flat, emptying rubbish, doing menial chores. It was good to be in the company of another person, especially one so good-natured and unstinting with her affection. The day passed and that night she became my lover.

Her clothes were threadbare and impregnated with dirt, so I gave her two thousand kroner to buy new ones. She returned with T-shirts, jeans and a windproof cotton jacket in bright green from the men's departments of Fotex and Daells Varehus. She'd also bought felt-tipped pens and a pad of drawing paper. Among the shop-new plastic bags were other bags retrieved from dustbins containing crushed Coca-Cola cans, polystyrene cups, and used drinking straws.

'People throw such good stuff away.' She held up her treasures for my inspection. 'We must keep them on the windowsill for luck and your return to health.'

'If you absolutely insist,' I laughed. 'But wash them first. They're full of germs.'

While I cooked, she produced sheet after sheet of naive drawings – winged figures floating over buildings, flowers with smiling faces – which she ran to show me. I made approving noises, playing the loving parent. I had never been so happy before. Since her arrival, even the weather showed another face, the sky bursting into blue. A mother duck swam proudly on the lake with nine babies in tow. Not all of them survived.

When my home-help and nurse returned from their holidays, all hell broke loose.

'We can't continue the service if you live with an able-bodied adult who isn't working herself and is capable of looking after you.'

There was a set-to over the debris on the windowsill, and my decision to let Camilla keep her charms did not impress them.

They lectured to me about people worse off who needed them more.

'That's OK,' I told them. 'I'll withdraw my claim for help and pay you what I owe until the end of the month. It's not a problem.'

But for them it was. They insisted on writing reports and discussing me with their supervisors. I was not behaving according to expectation and had to be taken to task. My friends were not much better.

'This girl is exploiting you,' they said. 'You might not think so, but it's obvious to us. She's unstable and you're at risk living with her.'

'Let me be the judge of that. I'm not dead yet. Why shouldn't I have a young lover to sweeten what's left of my life?'

'She's a drain on your finances.'

'Who else should I spend my money on?'

'She could up and go any minute. You must give some thought to the future.'

'You mean I should save for my funeral. Don't look so shocked, I've made provision for that. None of you will be financially encumbered.'

My social circle dwindled until Camilla and I were left in splendid isolation, but I didn't care. My life overflowed with laughter and pleasure. I read aloud, her head on my lap. She rearranged my furniture in the pattern of a cross. It was most inconvenient, but so what? It was an act of love and geometry. Other people were crazy, not us. Reality was a bore. The flat became festooned with ring-pulls picked up off the pavement and threaded on to tooth floss. We wrote love poems on toilet paper before using it for its intended purpose. We saved melon pips which she arranged in spiral patterns on the floor, exhorting me not to disturb them. From time to time I had to stand at the centre of the spirals while she laid hands on me, intoning a wordless melody.

Time passed. By the end of July, the heat became scorching and my flat oppressive. The atmosphere between us soured almost overnight. There was no keeping her indoors any more. She disappeared early in the morning and came back late, her skin salty with sea and sweat. A note of brutality entered our love-making, once so tentative and full of appreciation. I could tell she was getting impatient with my illness now that her efforts to cure me by magic had failed.

I became jealous, demanding to know what she did all day, where she went, and whom she saw. I started begging her not to leave me. I didn't want to let her out of my sight. The more I nagged, the further she went, the longer she stayed away.

She left a mess for me to tidy up and ignored my dietary needs, buying tinned food which I couldn't eat. When I complained, she snarled. I began to feel both afraid of her and afraid of losing her. I wanted her to stay and be my deathbed companion, but I also wanted her to go and leave me in peace.

Her reclaimed treasures had lost their childish innocence, a rusty knife, mutilated child's pram, and headless doll arriving in rapid succession. Surrounded by other people's rubbish, I felt I was going insane. Was this a fitting finish for a pointless life? If so, please God, let it end quickly.

I made up my mind to face death alone. That was, after all, what I'd been resigned to doing before she came along. So I screwed up my courage, and told her to go.

But she refused. 'I'll go when you're better.'

'Please don't play games with me. You know that'll never be.'

'I'm not playing games!' She threw me a look which was imploring and furious, defiant and helpless.

'There are hostels where you could stay. I'll help you with your benefit claims.'

'Don't you like me any more?'

'I love you. But we can't carry on like this. Look, as long as I'm alive, you can visit me every day if you want to. But you must see that I can't live with you much longer.'

'Why not?'

'Please don't do this!'

'I don't want to visit. I want to stay until you're better.'

I did not have the strength to fight. At night she took up a starfish position in my bed, pushing me up against the wall. She kicked and ground her teeth in her sleep. I took more and more sleeping tablets to blot out the horror of it all. I took them during the day as well, to while away the empty hours.

One morning she went out and didn't return for two days. Instead of being relieved, I was beside myself with grief. I lay face to the wall, still as a stone, for all the time that she was gone. When she returned, smelling rank and unwashed, wearing purple silk jeans and a leather jacket with lots of zips, I rounded on her.

'You've been turning tricks, haven't you?'

She stood in the middle of the room looking quite casual. But then, without warning, she lost it completely, overturning furniture and throwing everything in sight.

'Shh, I didn't mean it. Calm down. It's all right.'

When she ran out of steam, I managed to get her on to the bed where I held and rocked her while she sobbed her heart out. Later I made her a hot drink, undressed her like a baby, stroked her until she fell asleep. I took a sleeping tablet and lay in the dark until I drifted off myself. Eventually I awoke to the familiar routine of her fist between my legs, pumping without mercy into my groin.

The following morning she jumped out of bed with ominous determination. She helped herself to cereal, bringing her bowl into the bedroom and finishing off the last of the milk. Casting her eye briefly over the devastation from the previous night, she said: 'I'm going to give you a present and then I'm going. Either that or I'll kill you. It's up to you.'

I hardly registered what she said, but lay stony-faced, arms folded across my chest. I saw her go into the bathroom and heard her splashing about.

'Are you ready? I'm coming to give it to you now.'

When she came back draped in a towel, I leapt up in horror at the blood gushing from her slashed wrists.

'Here it is. You must drink.'

'Get away from me!'

'Drink!' She pulled my head back and forced her slashed wrist against my mouth. 'Drink.' She tugged at my hair until I opened my mouth and swallowed her blood. Funny thing is, once I started I couldn't stop. I didn't want to stop.

'Good. Now the other one!' I swallowed blood until I couldn't any more. At last she let go of my hair and returned to the bathroom. When she emerged, she was dressed, wrists bound with bloodstained bandages from the medicine chest.

'Goodbye. I'm going now.' She spoke as if we were polite acquaintances, as if she'd just stayed to tea. 'Thank you for having me.'

It took a while for me to recover. But when I roused myself, the first thing I did was gather the bloodied bedclothes, together with the accumulated junk, and throw the lot out. I threw out a load of other stuff as well, like things that were broken or didn't work properly, or just things that annoyed me. I put my furniture back in order, vacuumed and washed the floors. I didn't stop to think where all the energy was coming from.

There was no food in the flat, so I took a shower and went shopping. I hadn't walked in the street among people for over a year and marvelled at the bigness of everything. On the way back home, I bought an ice-cream, sitting on a bench by the lake to eat it. After all that blood, it tasted so sweet and milky, I started to giggle with growing hysteria. People stared at me.

Now it is November again and I'm still here. I don't bother keeping my hospital appointments any more. The doctors wrote me off ages ago, but I've outlived all their deadlines, so why should I believe a word they say? The sky is a glorious patchwork of blue with shades of grey reflected in the waters of the lake. I take the S-Train to stations along the coast and walk for miles. Next week I will use my funeral money to holiday in Crete. There are so many things I've not yet seen and done. If I'm still around next summer, I'll take the big boat from Nyhavn to Oslo and make my way to the land of the midnight sun. When my savings run out, I'm sure I'll find money from somewhere. I'm not thinking about it. I believe it will come to me.

CLAIRE LYNN

Travelling light

Tapped wheels ring true as horseshoes
all the length of the train.
I have folded my life into a bag
I stow on the rack overhead. Outside,
the platform shrinks like a shed skin.

Other passengers offer huge smiles
of seed-pocked watermelon;
help themselves to my age, family,
nation, salary. The floor slithers
with spat seeds as black as eyes.

In my head are the tunes
of an alien tongue. Even my name
is transmuted: back to front,
a brush-stroke landscape of forest
and mountain I pass through.

Twice I will wake
in a different place,
to scenery suddenly shifted.
Morning wipes from each window
the misted breath of the sleepers.

Out of water

She is naked as a fish
under the gown, her skin
scaly, saline.

She floats on morphine,
swims down corridors
of viscous light. Permits

the hooking of her wrist's
soft palate, gapes
at the drowning air.

He will part flesh
like curtains, lift
her backbone on the tip

of his fish-knife, ribs
unpicking like stitches.
She is filleted, cured.

Moving mountains

I

A billion ants lived
on a mountain top. One day
the mountain caught fire.
To survive, the ants
had to get down the mountain.
They gathered themselves
into a giant ball and rolled down.
Those on the outside
were burnt to death,
but the lives of many more
were saved.*

II

THIS IS LONDON.
This is Beijing.
This is Shanghai, Xi'an,
Chengdu, Changsha. This is
Yiyang, Xiangtan, Yueyang,
Huaihua.

These are my classmates.
This is my country.

*Story told by Chai Ling to students in Tiananmen Square in the early hours of
4 June 1989

III

We asked the girls to sew
the flowers; their fingers
are delicate. See how
the paper folds into petals,
each crisp white rose
brittle as bone, opening
wide as a heart. Each flower
threaded on black cotton.
We've made enough for everyone.
We scarcely know how many
we'll need. Will you wear
a flower for us? We've made
enough for everyone. All night
we worked by candlelight. How
could we have slept
last night? Now we have
flowers to fill baskets: white
and so light that none
are crushed.

IV

I stood apart at the gates,
watching them go, and I said
to one *Not you. You have a wife,
a child.* He stopped, and let me speak,
not with the power I have over him,
but man to man. *The time has passed
for this; things have gone too far.*
Last month I tied a flag to my handlebars
and rode alongside our students

with the other leaders, but now I say
The time for such actions
has long gone. I spoke
their names to him
like an incantation,
but he broke from me,
refurled his home-made banner
and ran after the bus.

V

It is noon, and the silence
between dormitories and dining-hall
is filled with the heat of the sun.
We who stayed behind
move through what shade there is;
each of us alone, invisible.
Passing, we cannot smile;
do not speak.

This morning's banners were white.
Last week's were red. Last week
we could not have imagined
what happened in Beijing
two nights ago. Today
we know nothing;
must start again.

VI

She tells a different story
from the news on the TV.
See the passion in her eyes,

in the movement of her hands.
Only the press of the crowd
holds up the bike on which she stands.

VII

Long ago there lived a Foolish Old Man;
two great mountains stood before his house,
almost blocking the road to his door.
One day he gathered his family together:

These two mountains in front of the door
are always in the way, whether we're coming
or going. Isn't it time they were moved?
His children and grandchildren all agreed.

Only his wife was doubtful: *You're already*
nearly ninety; you can't even lift a stone.
How will you shift these two great mountains?
Discarding the old woman's words, they set to work.

They weren't afraid to labour and toil;
they weren't afraid of the difficulties. Every day
they dug away at the mountains. The local Sage
saw them and laughed, said to the Foolish Old Man:

Look at yourself — you're so old, you can't pluck
the grass from the ground. So how are you going to move
these two huge mountains? The other listened,
smiling, said: *You haven't the sense of a child.*

I may die soon enough, but still there's my children.
My children will die, but then there'll be theirs.
With each generation, we'll be more and more numerous;
and the rocks of the mountain will be fewer and fewer.

Fish-bones

The tattoo parlour was lit by a single bulb. I stared at the half-drawn blinds, reluctant to watch the shiny needle pierce my skin. A neon light blinked outside the window, sending shards of blue flashing into the room.

Earlier in the evening, when I first met Dr 0 in Daisy's Tavern, he handed me his business card. I had read his name out loud, 'Dr 0'. I pronounced it 'Oh'.

He closed his heavy, blue-veined eyelids and said quietly, 'Zero. Not "Oh". Don't fucking say "Oh".'

It was the nativity scene tattooed on his bald head that first drew me to him. The colours were remarkably clear, but in my inebriated state I mistook a bright yellow star above the manger for the Star of David. I raised my glass to him, shouted 'Shalom!' and bought him the first of many whiskeys.

Several hours later, after we had drunk ourselves sober, we decided it was time to go to his tattoo parlour. For as long as I could remember, even as a young girl, I had wanted a tattoo. Black fish-bones: the simple, elongated, twisting skeleton of a fish. I used to know what it symbolised, but not any more, and certainly not then in the early hours of the morning.

Dr 0's grip on my arm was as tight as a tourniquet. I leaned back against the rigid spine of the chair in which I sat, while he concentrated on the needle pumping in and out of my red-dened wrist. The outline of black ribs wound across my wrist-bone and on top of my purple veins like a spiralling zipper. Pain cleared my whiskey-induced bravery.

'Do you think – shouldn't we use anaesthetic?'

Slowly he tipped his bald head back, scrolling through the wise men and the camels until I could see his black eyes. Then he looked down to his work without speaking. I could smell the alcohol emanating from both of our bodies. My sight blurred.

' Dr 0, do you have anything to drink?'

He straightened up and glanced around the room. I followed his gaze around the cluttered surfaces, over the stacks of dust-covered tattoo magazines and hand-sketched designs. His eyes swept the walls, hung with pictures of his masterpieces and awards from tattoo *aficionados*.

'Good idea.' He heaved himself out of his chair. His thick arms swung away from his leather-clad torso as he stomped toward the kitchen. It occurred to me that maybe I should be afraid of Dr 0, but I couldn't rouse any feelings of apprehension or concern.

I noticed an animal lying under a table. It was a cat, with long and matted fur and ears which were black and torn. I thought it might be dead, but then its eyes opened and shone. I spoke directly to it: 'You know, cat, tattoos aren't always a bad thing. They can be art, a permanent flesh painting.'

I looked at my inflamed wrist. The tattoo was taking shape; a flared tail-fin, spindly ribs, a rounded head with a vacant eye. To see it imprinted in my skin, finally, exhumed a strong sense of *déjà vu*. The refrigerator slammed. I heard a vehement curse; the floor reverberated and Dr 0 returned to the room.

I continued talking to the cat, since Dr 0 had become increasingly uncommunicative as the night progressed. 'Our skin, our flesh is so bare, so vulnerable. In a way, a tattoo becomes a timeless charm.'

Dr 0 didn't seem to notice my conversation with the cat, so I crouched next to it and shoved my wrist near its liquid eyes. 'Look, fish-bones. Something you'd like. A symbol of everlasting – something.' I lowered my voice and whispered near its ear. 'This is for my mother.'

The cat's ears were in bad shape and when I examined them closely, I saw they were tattooed with tiny birds, mice and lizards.

Dr 0 handed me a tin can full to the brim. I took a deep gulp and tasted vodka mixed with something unpleasantly thick and salty. I choked and resisted the urge to spit it on to the floor. 'I don't want to be ungrateful, Dr 0, but was there something in the can before you added the vodka?'

'Shit. Read the fucking label.'

I read the label out loud. '"String cut green beans."'

'And?' He held up his can for me to read.

'"Sweet white corn."' I looked at him, not sure I understood. 'You mean you mixed vegetables with vodka?'

'No. I dumped the fucking vegetables. But I figure I need vitamins, so I use the juice for drinks.'

'Oh, right. It makes an interesting cocktail, Dr 0. Thanks.'

Dr 0 sat on a low stool and picked up the needle. A mechanical hum began. The muscle in Dr 0's arm tightened and flexed.

I moved my head to try and see the tattoo that wrapped around his upper arm. There was a lot of red and cherubs and men with swords. 'Very medieval. What's the scene on your arm?'

'Don't you college kids ever read the Bible?'

'No, well not now, not in the classes I'm taking.'

'It's when the goddamn Romans murder all the first-born sons to find Jesus.'

Just what I wanted to look at. I turned to the table next to me and studied an ashtray full of greasy candy corns. Above it hung a torn reproduction of the infamous four dogs playing poker. The needle punctures shot slivers of pain up my arm. I took a healthy gulp of Dr 0's concoction and looked down. Entranced, I watched a drop of blood bubble up between my translucent hairs, wobbling there until Dr 0 blotted it with a stained rag made of denim.

Dr 0 moved his stool to the opposite side of my wrist and I scrutinised his other arm. I recognised this scene: Jesus rising from the dead. 'Easter. What is all this? Are you religious?'

'I read the Bible.'

'Roman Catholic, Protestant, Episcopalian? What are you?'

'None. That's bullshit. I just read the Bible.'

'An independent scholar. And do you believe it, Dr 0?'

'You don't?' He eyed me suspiciously.

'I believe it's biblical history, but . . . Well, you know, there've been many translations and it was written a long time ago.'

'History is history.'

'A lot of religions have –'

Dr 0 lowered his eyelids until all I could see was a slit of white. He clutched my wrist even tighter in his vice-like grip and my voice rose an octave. I changed the direction of our conversation. 'What other scenes do you have tattooed?'

'Moses, on my upper back, parting of the Red Sea on my arse. On my chest, the Creation of Man. My belly-button is the apple and my dick the serpent.'

'You're kidding.'

He began to unbutton his vest.

'No, no, I believe you. Really.'

He dropped the idea of disrobing and picked up the needle again. I took another guzzle and spilled the sticky drink down my chin and neck. 'I'm doing this for my mother.'

'Yeah? My first one was for my mother. See.'

He pointed to his arm. I looked, but all I could see was a long-haired Jesus wearing flowing robes in front of an open tomb, surrounded by angels. He tapped his arm impatiently and then I noticed in the centre of the scene, next to Jesus's halo, a heart with an arrow and the word, MOM, written in it.

'Nice. I don't mean like that exactly though, what I mean is that my mother has one also.'

'Mine too, a heart with my name. On her biceps.' He flexed his tattoos and stared out the window. 'Mom and me, we're close. We take a trip every year. She was going to Daisy's before I was born.'

I was jealous of Dr 0 and his mother. My mother had kept me at a distance all my life, as if she were afraid of me. I have never felt close to her.

Lifting the can to my lips, I took a drink, noticing at the bottom two kidney-shaped green beans floating towards my mouth. I jerked the can down and my lower lip caught on the edge. I touched my finger to my lip and then looked at my finger. It was smudged with blood and even though it didn't hurt, my eyes welled up with tears.

Dr 0 finished the tail-fin and stood up. I had no idea what

time it was in the real world, but I knew the sun was bound to rise soon and I was due to be at my family's for Thanksgiving Day.

I walked home in the dreary early-morning fog. It swirled around me, dreamlike, and I felt peaceful except for the throbbing of my wrist. Collapsing on the couch, I slept before heading to the holiday meal. I wore a long-sleeved dress with extra-long sleeves. The fabric rubbed against my wrist and the tattoo felt heavy, like an iron chain.

The house seemed to stand out brighter in the approaching dusk than I remembered. Moss-green house paint contrasted with the pink, camellia bushes blooming near the varnished door. Wiping my feet on the straw welcome mat, I noticed the WELCOME had worn off.

In the kitchen, my mother appeared small and frail after the largeness of Dr 0. I hovered near the counter, wanting to be near her, to see if she would feel something different. But everything was the same.

A harsh buzzer sounded and she grabbed a flowered potholder, reaching into the oven. The bare bulb from the oven shone on her face. Her shirt sleeve rose above her wrist, showing the aged, green numbers etched into her loose skin. I reached down, gently touching my own wrist.

LISA MATTHEWS

The ladies of Eastbourne

Six foot four in heels,
she stands next to me
at the plastic basins.
I comb my hair
while she lipstick kisses
the reflection's distance.
Then she stands to the side,
pulls her skirt
down her thighs
and asks for a light.

It's their first time here.
We talk about music,
clubs they could visit.

Somewhere there will be
blood on a kerb,
ticking *Mr* on the forms
at the A & E,
the why and the wherefore
the he or the she?

She'll lose control
of her bladder then.
Pushing the button
behind the water jug
she knows, and waits
for the nurse to come.
She knows –
she has no choice,
it's a bedpan
or the men's.

A Saturday morning

They sit at the counter
him in his hat
while the woman beside him
considers her nails.

The waiter pours coffee
and folds napkins into shape.
Bread in the ovens
continues to rise,
while someone looks on,
casts their eye over this.

Such a scene
such a morning
happens all the time.
And in the station nearby
they're unloading the mail,
somebody somewhere
has something to say.

My brother Frankie and other stories

That January the snow
had been falling for a month,
it was deep and getting deeper.
Mother stayed indoors,
she never liked the cold much.

We were not alone,
we were not unique.

Home entertainment
in the us–v.–them years,
meant babies or black eyes
and it was difficult to tell
sometimes, if they were
fucking or fighting next door.

We skinned rabbits
and drank beer when we could.
Frank wore the weather, heavy
like a wedding dress.
His affair with a salesman
was reaching its natural end.
He's older now
and mother knows.

That winter we played cards
at night, round the kitchen table
and wondered what kind of
piece of mind
a pile of matches could buy.

The last class visit

all our legs
came to the clearing
sit-here-Theresa took my coat
and dropped it

we stood, all of us
on all our legs
and watched the distance ahead
and the birds were singing

it's so large, she said
and leant on the arm
of a wooden bench

she looked at me
and saw my sister
I could hear the words
moving in her head

it was cold
it was morning
sit-here-Theresa
considered the edge

JULIA WIDDOWS

The quick and the dead

It was New Year's Day and we were attending the hamster's funeral. The air was coming straight from the Arctic and the children were giggling, excited, because burying the hamster meant that they could now have something else, and the something else they had in mind was a lizard with a ruff like a Jacobean lace collar. Only in green, and made out of skin. Or bright orange, and raised, when on the defensive.

I tried telling them that such animals only existed, free, in cereal packets. I told them that no self-respecting pet emporium would be open on New Year's Day, and that the Victorians observed deepest mourning for a whole year before permitting the normal routines and rituals of life, like marriage, to resume. And I felt that shipping in a lizard to take up residence on the sideboard, where Harald Hardrada the Hamster's cage still stood in desolate splendour, was akin to shipping in a new bride just to keep an eye on the children and satisfy the master's sexual needs. And no lizard worth its ruff would wish to be adopted on the rebound. I tried.

Dinny, my youngest, made a cross out of lolly sticks. He had been out to the newsagent's first thing and bought two ice lollies and selflessly eaten them all the way home, despite the freezing weather, in order to have two suitable sticks for a cross.

'Oh, Dinny!' I said, when I answered his twenty consecutive peals on the doorbell. 'Come inside quick. Your lips are blue.' He obligingly turned them inside out for me and said 'Daiquiri Scubas', but still consented to hug the radiator for warmth.

Shaq, my eldest, donated a little cardboard box, which we lined with blue tissue paper (left over from someone's Christmas present), and we gently lowered the stiff chestnut form of Harald Hardrada inside. He was cold, and oddly inanimate. For such a busy, quick (in every sense of the word) animal, it was a shock to see him curled, brittle and dry, like a very old autumn leaf, or one of those birds you step over in the gutter that you can never imagine as a real live flying thing.

I was glad that his eyes were closed, his wet blackcurrant eyes; and that his whiskers, which were always on the go, like the nozzle of a Hoover, were useless and still and invisible now.

I glanced up and caught Shaq's eyes gleaming a bit. But he counted himself too old for sentiment and turned away quickly and stuffed a biscuit in his mouth. 'I'm going up in the attic,' he mumbled.

'Whatever for?'

'Get the old fish-tank.'

'Whatever for?' I clutched Harald's cardboard coffin to my midriff.

'Make a great vivarium.' Easy come, easy go.

'No! Go and dig a hole first.'

Shaq and Tulip (middle child: see-saw, shuttlecock) banged the ringing earth with hand trowels, indulging in gravediggers' jokes. I could see them from the kitchen window, see their breath rising like tissue-paper bouquets, hear their fractured laughter.

'What we want,' they shouted, coming in, all bulk and static in their padded nylon coats, 'is a lizard. Or a gecko. They climb walls. You should see their tongues.' And Harald's mortal remains still lay on the kitchen table. *The bells of hell go ting-a-ling-a-ling, for you but not for me.*

Before Harald there had been fish. Before the fish there had been two mice who bred like rabbits. Before the mice, a kitten who got out into the road. One day there might be a dog, but not before everyone, including Dinny, is old enough to walk it daily. Not me. Not me. I've had my heart tugged, and my hands in the shit, clearing up, too often.

I had a cup of coffee, and then it was time. 'Get Dad. Dinny, coat!'

Tulip brought a twist of turquoise velvet flowers she'd had as a bridesmaid last summer. They were all that remained of her head-dress. We laid a blanket of blue tissue over Harald, folded it back, just as if he was in bed, and rested the flowers on top. There was no lid to his box. The cold lumps of earth would go right over his whiskers, pressing the lids down on his liquefying eyes. I suppose it didn't matter.

We marched out into the cold.

'Don't laugh!'

Tulip kicked Shaq; Shaq kicked Dinny. There were elbows everywhere. Their father was no help, looking like 'How long is this going to take?' and hunching his shoulders and surveying the house wall for whispers of structural damage he would have to shore up come the milder weather.

'Take this hamster,' I said, 'into Your care, Jesus. Thank You for his life. And look after him in death.'

'Amen.'

Snort.

'Amen.'

Gobbets of swallowed laughter. Honking. Tears streaming. Shaq bending over and holding his aching stomach. Good. Serve him right. Hope it hurts.

Tulip crouches down and strokes the earth flat over the hole with the back of her trowel, like she was stroking a cat with a sore back. Her mouth a ripe plum. One day, in a life I cannot imagine, she will be a good-looking woman; ten thousand years hence, as far away as the ten thousand years ago, before she was born.

We stand in the cold back garden, them thinking about lizards with exotic ruffs, him thinking of the cracks in the exterior plaster, me thinking: oh grave, where is thy victory?

Dinny plants his cross. He hasn't put on his coat, but his brother's thick checked shirt, so there will probably be a row when Shaq gets round to noticing. On the horizontal bar of the cross there is a joke: Q: *What's orange and walks upright*? A: *A human bean*. Dinny stands up again, with his head bowed and his hands clasped in front of him, like he has seen on television.

'Goodbye, Harald,' I say. 'Sleep well.' And then: 'Let's get indoors, it's bloody freezing.'

So later, when we hear that an old, old friend of ours has died, been killed in a car crash on the way home from a New Year party – not drunk, not drunk at all, but skidded on some ice – I know the day will be fixed. Fixed. Out of all the twenty thousand years of days, this will be remembered: the day we buried the hamster, the day we lost our friend, the first one of us to die. Someone our age. Child-bearing age. Not a distant relative or an old person. Someone with bright eyes and busy whiskers.

I took the cage off the sideboard. I helped Shaq climb into the attic. I dusted the sides of the fish-tank for reliques of old algae and guppy kiss-prints. I promised: 'Tomorrow. Tomorrow we will go to the pet emporium. Tomorrow we will go to the library and find out all there is to know about keeping lizards happy. We can do nothing more today. Today is New Year's Day.'

'What about the Victorians?' asks Tulip.

'They were Victorians,' I reply.

Suzanne Batty

A lesson in twins

It's their doubleness I dislike.
Bad enough the sullen innocence
of one. They smell of eagerness.
Too clever by two halves. Godless.
Matching frocks run up from old
curtains. Shoes with too much sense.

They must learn to separate.
I let the bad one go. The other
sulks, climbs on a chair, clumsy
stands there for hours, hating.
Humiliated. There is hope for her.
She is martyred with a certain flair.

Two things

For one thing it was November
and 21 degrees. People idled about
in shorts and shades, nonchalant.

For another the sun's eclipse
was disappointing. Children lined
the streets looking straight up, rebellious.

Did they want scorched eyeballs
and blinding head pains?

Did they not want a future
of breathing apparatus and boot camps?

Joshua's poem

A month of skulls. The first, a bird's perhaps,
oddly warm in the hand. We are ice people
venturing out, wound round with clothes
and clothes. Dogwood and reeds bend
to a fallen sun. Josh pockets vertebrae
odd teeth, heads. He has been fretting all day
over God.

The baby is hauled through barbed wire
through thorns. Joshua points to a blue line
miles away, where we should be.
I am a reader of maps, a holder of hands
fraying his nerves. Today you're preferred.
The baby has a name for you, something like
Ice-a-nin, said loudly in gusts of air
so cold and dry it hurts to breathe in.

She is a fury, a wild cat, her brother
a caught fish who dangles from my skeleton.
We slide across a wooden walkway rotting
into marsh. He is clamped to my thigh shouting
the cows are going to get us! and
smoking makes you die!

But they won't, those cows, we'll just pretend
they're ghosts and track the frozen swirls of dung
to reach the river. Josh is jumping from stiff grass

to hard mud spiriting bony legs along
amongst corpses. A sheep's head is all holes. Horns.
A toothy jaw. A bird's backbone.
It's all right, he yells, it's just a dinosaur!

We drag them back in a baker's crate
with piles of wood. Lights sway on the cliffs.
Our house is an old woman's house, rocking.
The tremble of coronation plates, the flutter of lace.
Stiff chairs hold old people's shapes. Ships' masts
are burning and frosty reeds; a footpath sign imprinted
with birds that gurgle at dusk. Outside the gorse
clenches branches like thick gloves.

There is Irish dancing in the parlour
a blazing cake in the kitchen where we sing
Happy Birthday Jesus, though Josh declares
he's an unbeliever. The tree-lights glow
through a veil of ash, the house is humming
with sulphur and wood-smoke.

From the chilly upstairs Josh shouts through the dark
I've seen them! the dinosaurs! I knew they'd come back!
and we run to look through the smoky glass, see
an early moon, ghostly creatures with huge white horns,
a sledge spilling over with blue-white bones.

Incidents at Grindleford

She is carrying a swan under her arm
like a briefcase. Or she is at a bus stop
with little canvas shoes letting in rain.

As she walks I hear the creaking of her
chest. The sky is bigger than the ground.

She sits in a stone circle, cross-legged,
eating yoghurt. The roads have been blocked
by snow. No cars. Only icy tunnels
where people have burrowed through.

She strides along the ridge like a twin
with the snow curving over.

She drinks like a slow fish
down in the valley
under the toothy rocks.

Dreams of warthogs

I am one of those bad girls who converses
with dirt, snuffling in the shrubbery.
I do the same thing over and over.
I am pricking out seeds, weighed down
by summer's gaping terror. I am
cultivating a horror of blue hydrangeas.

I find myself asleep in a blue room
a stored corpse decomposing in my
attic, a spade gleaming in my luminous
yard. I am selling all my clothes
in underground tunnels, becoming
naked and thin in a roar of stale air.

I once lived with warthogs in a dark hut
and pissed outside in the cloud forest's
steam where the idle paparazzi flashed
like glow-worms. Drove my father's car
through tangles of snakes, the florescence
of spiders floundering on vinyl seats.

I was a bad child with rage bent backwards.
I am an empty pram. I am walking uphill,
over and over, through damp clouds descending.
Past heartless rocks that cough and creak,
the blow and hiss of the distant sea. And overhead,
swarms of oyster-catchers sharpening their beaks.

JANE WOOD

The girl who
turned to stone

'You're going to stay at Auntie Babs'. Auntie Babs' and Uncle Eric's. I told you that.' Mummy stands with her back to the sink. Kate and Ellen sit at the table. Ellen's mouth is open. She can't believe what Mummy's saying.

'I can't look after you if I'm in the hospital. How can I? And Daddy must go to his work.' She's holding a tea-towel. There's pictures on it: apple trees and a round building with a pointy roof. She hooks the tea-towel on to its peg and bends to rattle something on the boiler. The coke sighs and sinks. The circle of heat gets hotter.

'It won't be for long. And when you get back there'll be a surprise.'

She stands upright, arching her back. She puts her hand to the small of her back and rubs. Her stomach billows into a full sail. It's like in the picture labelled BOAT, the one in Ellen's picture book.

60

Ellen doesn't want a surprise. And she doesn't like Mummy being a boat. She never used to be one. And she never used to say what she's saying now: 'You're going to Auntie Babs'. I know you don't want to. But it's the best we can do.'

They've been got ready. They've got their coats on. But it can't be happening. It's not what happens in Ellen's life. She's never put her coat on for a thing like this. When she puts her coat on it's to go to the shops. First they go to the grocer's shop, where the man cuts cheese with a wire, and bacon with a bacon-slicer. Then they go to the bread shop with its warm smell and the lady who shouts on account of her deafness. And the lady gives Ellen a glacé cherry, which she eats because Mummy said it's the polite thing to do. Then they go to the greengrocer's. And on the way home Ellen walks on the little pink wall, her hand in Mummy's hand. She lifts her feet carefully and puts them down carefully. And if her legs wobble Mummy squeezes her hand. And she does not fall. They come home to the warm kitchen with the coke boiler. And rice pudding for tea with jam on top. And when Daddy comes home, there's a bath and a story and bed.

Mummy never said that this was not for ever. That there would come a time when they would part. When Mummy would throw her off to someone like Uncle Eric, with his yellowy face and his black-rimmed glasses.

Ellen's eyes are filling.

'Don't cry.' Mummy comes and puts a hand either side of Ellen's face. 'Don't cry, my poppet. Don't break my heart.'

Ellen's a good girl. But what can she do? What can she do when Mummy suddenly looks like a boat and is saying these terrible things?

She can freeze, that's what she can do. She can become a

statue. That way Ellen isn't Ellen. She has no real face, no real skin to feel Mummy's hands. And Mummy mustn't mind the tears that have already come. They came before she froze her eyes, before she knew that tears could break her mummy's heart.

'Oh, don't,' says Mummy, as she wipes away tears of her own.

She puts out her arms and gathers Ellen in. She hugs, all warm and nice, stroking Ellen's hair. Which makes things difficult. But Ellen keeps a hold. Keeps her eyes as stone. Keeps the tears at bay.

Mummy lets go. Sits back. Is smiling. 'Oh, dear,' she says. 'Kate, fetch my hankie.' And Kate, who is older than Ellen and not crying, opens the stiff catch on the top of Mummy's bag and lets out the sweet smell of face powder that lies alongside Mummy's purse and Mummy's keys.

Mummy blows her nose. 'Oh dear, oh dear. What a fuss we're making.' And she laughs. She really does. As though that's over, done with, cleared away.

'Draw me a picture,' she says. 'In the hospital I'll put it by my bed and think of you.'

Kate picks up a crayon and draws the black square she always draws, with the black triangle on top of it. It's a house, with a thin rectangular chimney, square windows and a door.

Mummy checks inside her handbag, then checks inside the small brown suitcase that's been packed for weeks and waiting in the hall. She's all smiles.

'Will it be sweets?' Kate asks.

'Will what be sweets?'

'The surprise.'

'No, not sweets, my darling.' And Mummy laughs. A laugh that holds its secret tight within it.

Ellen can't draw houses. So she picks up the purple crayon and drags it round the paper. She drags it slowly at first. It's a big wax crayon. It's making purple spirals. They start large then get smaller. They get smaller and smaller and harder and harder, until the dot in the centre is the hard hurting spot in her heart. And the crayon goes through the hard hurting spot in her heart and leaves its mark on the table.

'Ellen!' Mummy's cross.

In the car, Ellen looks at Kate to see what Kate is doing. Kate's rubbing her hand on the seat. She's finding out how it feels. Then she bounces up and down.

'Stop jumping around in the back.'

It's the first thing Uncle Eric has said. Ellen looks at the top of his head, at that silly spot where he's got no hair. Uncle Eric's really got too much hair, but it's all in the wrong places. He has black hairs coming out of his nose and his ears. And dots of it trying to come out on his chin. And he's oily and yellow and he wears brown suits. And the touch of him would be slippery as butter.

She wants to tell him: 'It wasn't me, I wasn't bouncing'. But he might get angry. He's all scrunched up and gripping the wheel.

Kate says, 'Can't we go any faster?'

Ellen is listening to Kate so as not to think about Mummy. Uncle Eric takes a long time to turn into the main road.

Kate says, 'Do you like mint humbugs?'

Uncle Eric doesn't answer. He says, 'Better safe than sorry.'

'We've got a jar of them at home,' Kate's telling him. 'We keep it on a shelf in the kitchen.'

Ellen is listening to Kate so as not to think about Mummy

standing by the gate and waving her hand. About her getting smaller and smaller. About how, if she kept getting smaller and smaller, she'd shrivel away into nothing at all.

Uncle Eric's not listening to Kate. So Kate stops talking to him.

Ellen thinks of mint humbugs so as not to think about Mummy. She thinks of mint humbugs then she thinks about humming. That's what the car is doing. A long drawn out sort of hum. Stretchy. Like crêpe paper. She starts saying 'mint humbug' over and over into the hum. Kate tells her to stop it, but she doesn't stop it. She just moves it to the inside of her head, where Kate can't hear it.

They go down streets. She looks at the streets. Then it's fields. And she looks at the fields. And all the time she's saying 'mint humbug'. And all the time she's trying hard not to think about Mummy.

Uncle Eric says, 'It was a last-minute thing.' Ellen looks at Kate to see if Kate can understand what he's saying. But Kate's gone to sleep. 'You were supposed to go to Sylvia's. But Bert took ill.'

Ellen tries to think of something to say, but Uncle Eric thinks she's said something already. 'I can't hear you over the engine,' he says.

She keeps saying 'humbug'. But that's inside her head. He can't hear that either.

The suitcase is put in the passage and the coats are put on the pegs. Kate and Ellen are put in a room. Uncle Eric leaves them there. He says he has things to see to. Ellen listens for his footsteps going away. But she doesn't hear them. So she thinks he's still there, standing very quietly outside the door.

There's a settee and two armchairs in the room. And a pile of magazines on a coffee table. Someone has placed the magazines on the exact centre spot of the table. Which means that they mustn't be touched.

'There's no toys,' whispers Kate.

No toys, thinks Ellen. She doesn't like it that Kate whispers. But she knows why she does it. It's the room. The room's watching them. It wants to see what they'll do.

Kate sits in an armchair. She bounces, but only once. Then she sits still. Ellen knows why she sits still. The room didn't like her bouncing. The room said: 'Sit still and shut up'. It's watching for what they do wrong. It makes Ellen hold on to her breath. She looks out of the window. A big red bus goes by.

Behind her Uncle Eric is suddenly there. He comes round in front of her and shuts the curtains. He's standing too close. He says: 'When Barbara comes back, we'll have tea.'

He looks at her, wanting her to speak. But she can't speak. She doesn't know who Barbara is. And she's holding her breath because of the room. She shouldn't be here. She should be at home. She should be in the bath by now, closing her eyes. And Mummy should be pouring the water over her head to get the shampoo off. She should be feeling the towel hard on her head, then soft on her eyes. She should be opening her eyes and seeing Mummy. Not Uncle Eric standing like he is, like he doesn't know what to do next. Like he's expecting her to tell him. What can she tell him?

She doesn't like Uncle Eric. She doesn't like the way he looks. She doesn't like his face. He doesn't want them here. The room doesn't want them and he doesn't want them. He doesn't want Kate. And he doesn't want Ellen. And he doesn't know what to do next. And he wants her to say something. But she can't. She's holding her breath. And if she didn't hold her breath she'd cry. And that would be a fuss. And Uncle Eric wouldn't know what to do with a fuss. He might come and touch her with his slippery hands. He might try a hug. And then she'd have to scream. Which would be impolite. And he'd tell Auntie Babs. And Auntie Babs would tell Mummy. And Mummy'd be sad that she'd made a fuss. And Mummy'd not love her.

Uncle Eric coughs. He rubs his hands together. He says it's cold, do they want a fire? Ellen doesn't know if they want a fire. She fixes her eyes on the curtains. Roses, in lines. Big red roses, set against pink. Uncle Eric's roses. Mustn't think about them. The walls are closing in. Getting too close. He's too close. Mustn't think about walls. Or breathing. Breathing too loud. Or Mummy. Or butter. Or slippery things.

Kate wants to cry. Ellen suddenly knows it. Mustn't think about crying. Mustn't think about Kate. Nothing. Must think about nothing. Nothing at all. Must stand very still and think about nothing. Think about nothing and nothing. Nothing, nothing. Over and over. Just the one word. Stretching it out; stretching the word out and all over. Turning it grey, like a grey blanket. A blanket of stone. The stone of a statue.

They think she's here. But she's not. They're here. Kate. Uncle Eric. But she's not, she's not here. What's here is the grey thing, the dumb thing, the stone thing. The nothing.

There's a drumming in her ears and she can barely hear Kate saying, 'No, thank you', about the fire, very quietly from her armchair. Uncle Eric turns his attention to Kate. He says 'Well', and rubs his hands again. But he keeps standing there. He keeps not knowing what to do next. And Ellen can feel Kate wanting to cry. And she'd like to tell her 'Kate, turn to stone', but

Ellen's turned to stone, so Ellen can't tell her. Stone doesn't talk.

Uncle Eric mumbles and moves and gets to the door. 'Well, we'll have tea soon as Barbara – She won't be long.'

Auntie Babs bumps right into him as she comes through the door. She's using her stick. And her stick hits Uncle Eric hard on the ankle. Kate nearly laughs. Auntie Babs walks stiffly. They're supposed to feel sorry because she walks stiffly. But Ellen can't feel sorry because of her smile. It's a thin red smile and it's hard to know what Auntie Babs means by it. She uses it now as she asks them, 'So, what have you two been doing?'

She doesn't wait for an answer. She turns to Uncle Eric. 'Eric, have you made up the beds?' Then she turns back to them. 'We weren't expecting you. We've got nothing in.' She takes off her hat. It's a pink hat. It's unlike any hat Ellen's seen Mummy wear.

'I suppose you like cake.' Auntie Babs is looking at Kate. She expects Kate to answer.

Kate whispers, 'Yes, thank you.'

'Speak up, I can't hear you.'

'Yes, I like cake,' Kate almost shouts.

'Good. That's better. And you?'

Ellen wants to know what sort of cake. But she can't ask.

'Cat got your tongue?' Auntie Babs laughs. Uncle Eric hovers. There's a long silence. Then Kate say, 'She likes chocolate cake.'

After that it's all right. She doesn't have to say anything. She doesn't have to say anything for the whole time they're there. If something needs saying, Kate says it for her. And nobody minds. Nobody notices.

And when she gets home Mummy's happy to see her. And so's Daddy. The surprise is a baby. It's a nice baby. It's called Mary Jo.

Mummy is changing its nappy when she says, 'Auntie Babs was very pleased with you. She said how quiet and well-behaved you both were.' Mummy is proud. Ellen is happy. Now she can put the visit behind her.

But Kate says, 'Ellen didn't speak. Never. Not once. I had to speak for her.'

Mummy has the nappy-pin in her mouth. She looks at Ellen. She looks concerned. Ellen's heart shivers. But when Mummy takes the pin out of her mouth it's only to say, 'Well, she's speaking now. So, there's no harm done.'

There's no harm done. And everything goes back to normal. Except now it's Mummy, Kate, Ellen and the baby who go to the shops. Everyone likes the baby. The lady from the bread shop even comes out from behind her counter and into the street to see it in its pram. She shouts its name to it under the hood, and sets it crying. And in all the excitement she forgets to give Ellen a cherry.

There isn't time to walk on the little pink wall. They have to hurry home and get the baby fed. And she can't hold Mummy's hand because Mummy needs both her hands for the pram. And Mummy can't sit, after lunch, telling stories. Babies are work, Mummy says. But it's all right, Ellen understands that. She knows to keep out of the way. She's quite happy. And a trouble to no one.

Ellen's up at the top of the garden, by the plum tree, where the grass is long. She's been there all afternoon. She's digging a hole. She scrapes mud from the hole. It's special mud: sunset orange. Mummy's so busy she doesn't have time to turn round. So Ellen will make her a present. She holds the mud in her hands. It's warm in her hands. And as she moulds it she can feel it drawing the sounds of the garden in: the buzz of the bee, the drone of heat, the swish of the long grasses, Kate's boasts as she cartwheels, Daddy's cough. It sucks them all up.

She smooths it into a ball. She's going to tell Mummy to keep it in the bathroom, by the hot-water tank. To keep it alive.

Mummy's voice sounds from the bottom of the garden, like a lullaby. It comforts the goldenrod and the marigolds, it praises the delphiniums. It's Mummy's voice rocking the cradle of the garden with the sound of Ellen's name. She takes Mummy's lullaby voice and smooths it over the mud. And turns it from mud into the bright golden orb in her story book.

She runs to Mummy and opens her hands. 'See, Mummy. See how I hold and soothe and stroke and guard. See, Mummy. See how it gleams.'

But no, Mummy can't see, not without Ellen saying the words. And before she can say the words Mummy says, 'Throw that mud on the garden and wash your hands for tea.'

Mummy is blind to the golden orb. And it's no good saying the words – 'Mummy, I put everything in. Mummy I made it for you' – if Mummy can't see it.

'Don't start,' Mummy says. She sounds tired. 'Put it down,' Mummy says, and her voice is as soft and precise and as cold as a frost pattern on a window pane. But Ellen stands her ground. She doesn't look at Mummy now. Instead she stands like a great stone lump rooted in concrete on the kitchen step.

H e l l o

You are standing in a roadside phone-box.
I am standing in my hallway
listening to the swish of distant traffic.

I think of your beard, your dark jacket,
the dazzle of undipped headlights
catching the slanting rain.

We are talking about whatever it is
you say you are calling me for,
something and nothing.

I am plucking petals from orange marigolds
in the jug on the windowsill in the hallway,
putting other words in your mouth.

I think of you standing in the phone-box
fingering shapes on the wet glass,
the curve of your penis, your belly,
you standing sipping coffee after love.

V e s s e l

I

To my surprise you manhandle the canoe
prow-first into the water.

I would have had us lower her gently
down the rushy bank.

I like to feel you shifting behind me.
The wind carries away my voice.

We drift under low bridges, wild cherry.
Kingcups glow under the larches.

Cattle browse at the water's edge.
Cleopatra trails her hand through the weeds.

II

We startle the grey goose
from her round nest.

Our island, like all such islands,
bristles with spears, whispers.

We peel oranges, break and eat
each segment carefully.

I collect ferns and mosses.
You mark the boundaries of our fire.

The soil weeps rust-red stains
over the white rocks.

III

This garage needs a clear-out, he says.
All berths are temporary.

She studiously ignores
the upturned vessel under the sycamores.

How pretty. The hangman has let
the clematis get entangled in his noose.

The bruise at the side of my mouth
is becoming the colour of thunder.

I see you are home already.
I am buried under sand.

IV

Rimini. The waiter crosses the marble floor.
You turn each peach in the bowl of iced water.

By that fountain in the Alpujarras,
arum lilies. Old men reminiscing. Franco's Spain.

She waters the garden with a small can.
Sometimes a whole morning passes this way.

Blue dragonflies hatch and mate within the hour.
Love-lies-bleeding under the apple tree.

You are learning the art of opening oysters,
the systole and diastole of anemones.

V

She has sunk his boat behind the roses,
filled it with carp.

He pushes the hard glass
against my closed lips.

She remembers the way he mewed
like a kitten.

I swallow our unborn children.
Milk and salt.

Foxgloves. A stone heron.
Such gifts you bring me.

S u n d a y   a f t e r n o o n
i n   M o o s o n e e

Chilly Willy's is changing hands.
The liquor store is closed.

In the Metis and Non-Status Indian
Association souvenir shop,
I take refuge from sharp rain.

I browse through the T-shirts,
re-fold wolves with blue eyes.

Girls tidy tamarack geese,
stack hide slippers,

remark that a small soapstone carving
might sell as a holder for toothpicks.

Not much doing, out on First Street.

Besides the odd tourist
with a damp, flapping map:

a woman hauling a buggy
up the steps of Christ the King,

a boy with a smile
as vacant and wide as the Moose River,

children making mud-pies

and a husky in moult
outside a shack scrawled *Fuck You*.

I walk to the waterfront.

You sure don't belong here,
you sure don't belong here,
says the man in the freighter canoe.

Linda Leatherbarrow

L *a*   L *u n a*

Tomorrow we're going to Macy's and I'm going to buy something on every floor. Already we're holding hands, snuffing up
the warm sweet air like dogs catching a long-forgotten scent.
We stand on the corner of Herald Square, taking it all in, then
follow the map to the hotel.

It's a good hotel but not grand: a canopy over the street so
you can make it from the cab without getting wet, but no door-
man; a certain amount of marble in the lobby, but no real
opulence. A compromise that suits us both.

'Credit card, sir.'

Rick opens his wallet, hands one over, and we wait while the
desk clerk taps into the computer. There is that moment as
always, that clutches at the heart, but everything checks out
and we take the lift to the fourteenth. In Las Vegas, the hotel
was topped by a neon cowboy whirling a rope of stars; in Miami
it was simply brash, in Savannah colonial. In between, we

roughed it: trailer parks, empty summer shacks, easy-to-break-into long-abandoned farmhouses high in the Appalachians. In one place, in a cupboard, we found a .22 rifle. I took a photo of Rick standing on the porch with the gun in his hand.

'Don't smile,' I said. 'Scowl.'

Pulling the hip-flask out of my pocket, I take a swallow. In this room there are sachets of coffee by the coffee machine; a shower that works; body lotion, shampoo, cakes of Pears soap, thick white towels; and a wide bed you could make love on all night long, a bed we negotiate like honeymooners, nervously laying out our clothes and sitting on its edge.

The last bed back home was four-poster pine, first twelve months free, no deposit. They've probably taken it already. And the telly, and the sofa, and the rest. I can't remember how many homes we've set up. Suddenly I think of the house in Bristol, us going off quietly one morning as if we were just going shopping, the garden full of freezers and fridges jam-packed with frozen crab-meat, scampi, lobsters, octopus, a lash-up of wires trailing across the lawn, the whole garden humming.

There are musicians in the next room. They practise for an hour – saxophone and penny whistle – then go out. Thoughtfully arranged on the table-top is a subway map and a magazine full of restaurant reviews. I leaf through the magazine while Rick's in the bathroom. Down below the wind churns through deep stone canyons, past the cast-iron buildings, the Chrysler and the Flat Iron. Sirens. I can't keep away from the window. Lights slip over the big buildings, fish over rocks. It makes me happy. There's nothing worse than wind blowing through trees.

'You hungry?'

Rick has showered and his hair lies slicked against his head. His skull goes down flat at the back to his neck. My father's head was dolichocephalic, a bean sticking out on a pin. He used to cycle to the pub, his head gliding smoothly above the hedges. Three heads wins the lady a china clown.

Rick is looking at me, impatient.

'Ravenous,' I tell him.

He opens his wallet again, pulls out the credit card, lays it on the palm of his hand, and wiggles it so the little hologram eagle flies. 'Three more days. If we're careful. Ready?'

'Ready.'

When we set out, his wallet was fat with cards, a flock of eagles. Now there's only one. He stows it away, then comes across and holds me. I say nothing about the three days, though it comes as a surprise. I want to tell him, I love you. He strokes my hair. Last time we had sex, I curled into his side and told him I adored him. Funny old-fashioned word.

'I don't want to be adored,' he said.

Quite right, but just the same it hurt. My father used to brush out of the house while my mother stood there, eyes full of tears. 'Your coat,' she'd say. 'Your coat.'

He'd slam down the hill without it, the weight of her love hanging in the house, muffling me into a silence I couldn't break.

'Indian?' Rick says. 'Thai? Greek?'

'Italian.'

La Luna lies at the south end of Mulberry Street, where Little Italy merges with China Town, where the jewellers' shops glow with trinkets: frogs, dogs, rats, a dinky golden car, easily transportable wealth, one step up from having your teeth filled with gold. 'Never sell,' said my mother. 'Always pawn.'

La Luna is just past Umberto's Clam House. 'Where,' I tell Rick, quoting from the magazine and pointing at the bullet-holes in the window frame, 'Joe "Crazy Joey" Gallo was shot dead in 1979.'

Rick doesn't respond.

Beside the doors, there's a plastic Bambi half hidden by a barrel of daffodils. I give it a pat on the head. Last year we raised fifteen thousand pounds with a start-up business loan from Leicester City Council when Leicester was City of the Environment. Recycled plastic to be turned into fence-posts. I wasn't sorry to leave Leicester, wasn't sorry to leave Bristol, but leaving the last house was a downer. I'd almost got to know the neighbours. Rick ruffles the daffodils. 'Sure you won't change your mind?'

We'd had a tiff on the subway. Rick wanting something grander, me saying I'd rather stretch it and have the three days. La Luna has no bullet-holes, no flowers, only a shrivelled arti-choke on a plate in the window, a heap of tagliatelle the colour of hoover dust. 'Honest and unassuming,' the review said.

'A dump,' says Rick.

Instantly, I'm depressed, my shoulders stiffen with effort. The whole street looks tacky. Taking a quick swig from my flask, I think: This could be the last time you do this. But that's stupid. There's always going to be restaurants with Rick. In the Camden house we didn't even have a cooker.

Rick holds out his hand and I pass the flask over. He tips his head right up, takes a long drink, then gives it back.

'After you.'

La Luna appears to be the same as it was when it first started out: the benches battered, the tables rickety, the mural along one wall cracked and peeling. I can't imagine why I insisted on coming here. All this continuity and looking back, it drives me nuts.

'Australian?' croaks the waitress from smoke-charred lungs.

'London.'

'Ah, London. You gotta spotted dick? My niece, come back from England, said she ate spotted dick. You eat spotted dick?'

'Not all the time,' says Rick. He's wittier than me. When I make a joke it's not expected and can pass unnoticed, my puns seem accidental, my *doubles entendres* mistakes.

'It's good?' says the waitress.

Her face beneath the heavy make-up is too old to be pretty. Forty, I think, coming up for forty; a little bitter with it all, sad and angry under the smile. No way am I going to be working when I'm old.

'Very good,' says Rick, smiling back.

'You wanna sit here?' She shows us to a table right at the back in a room off the main room.

'I'd rather be at the front.'

'Here's quiet.'

'I don't want quiet. I want to be with the action.'

'You want action?' says the proprietor, butting in and taking over. 'You talk to her,' indicating the waitress. 'She's action.'

He beckons us to a table inside the main room, clears away the remains of someone else's meal, exchanges the soiled cloth for a pristine white one, then waves us into seats which rock a little on the uneven cement floor. He looks round for the waitress. Shouts 'Maria!'

She brings over two glasses of water and sets them down; two plates, cutlery, napkins; a loaf of French bread; a bottle of olive oil.

'You lucky people,' he says, handing us a menu.

We choose while he waits.

'That it?'

He disappears and returns almost immediately. His look, as he lowers the carafe on to the table, is both condescending and battle-weary. He makes a tired movement with his hand that says 'Help yourself'. His trousers are torn and the top button on his fly is undone, his neck dotted with black moles.

Rick pours the wine and, just before he drinks, I stretch out my glass to his and we clink. I'm not superstitious, I can walk under ladders, but there are some things I don't care to miss out. Breaking off a piece of bread, I dunk it in oil.

'D'you know, I've never had oysters.'

'Oysters? They weren't on the menu.'

'I know, just saying.'

Near us, in a broken frame, is a blow-up copy of a testimonial from the Governor of Maine. All over the walls are photographs: starlets and comedians behind cracked glass. At the top end of the room, by the window, a big group is celebrating. Their laughter rolls back to us, edgy and abrasive. 'My mother was in the dream,' says our neighbour. 'Mother, flames, death, birth, blood.'

I take a big gulp of wine and instantly it lifts me up.

The proprietor returns with our salad. As he moves away, I notice the stitching has come undone on the back seam of his trouser seat. A little white shirt tail sticks out. 'Are the luckiest people in the world,' he sings, gravelling his voice like Satchmo's.

'*Il Patrone*,' says Rick, not knowing Italian, only guessing.

We eat strips of aubergine marinated in garlic and salt and get quickly drunk.

'I'll sort something out when we get back,' Rick says. 'I will, I mean it.' He reaches across and takes my hand. 'That's a promise.' I believe him and don't believe him, a trick I learned a long while ago; how to hold two opposites in my heart at the same time. Sometimes it makes me tired; sometimes it makes me quiet.

Il *Patrone* comes back and I wonder if he can see in our faces all the things that haven't worked out, wonder if he's thinking: another pair of losers, another pair of jerks. He whips the cutlery off our plates and lays it on the tablecloth again, lining it up as if it has never been used; then takes away our plates and comes back with two bowls of spaghetti drowned in thick crimson sauce. Rick's has slices of fried mushroom on top, otherwise they're identical. He places a jar of grated parmesan in front of us, showers black pepper over our bowls.

'You lucky, lucky people,' he says, then sighs and moves away between the other diners.

Maria stands at the back of the room, watching him in that unseeing way that tells me they are man and wife. Her legs are slender and her feet slipped into small tight shoes. Her toenails will be varnished tomato-sauce crimson and he will put his big freckled hands on her legs, slide them up over her shinbones, over her knees, and her eyes will be very distant, and his will be soft and wet. His hands will be clumsy.

'You wanna big one?' He's talking to two young women. 'You gotta big one.' They giggle. Moments later something large, long, and drowned in the same crimson sauce arrives. 'Big one,' he says. 'Enjoy.' This time, as he goes by, there is white flour on his trousers.

When the bill comes, Rick lays the card on the saucer and I watch Maria whisk it away. The name on this one is J. M. Bird.

Rick signed it back in London and I remember wondering if J. M. Bird was Janice or Julian.

When we come out, the trees are lit up with fairy-lights. The other restaurants have flowers on the tables, glitzy mirrors, cane chairs, waiters in crisp uniforms giving us the hard sell as we pass along.

'Hey, Frank,' yells a heavy blonde woman, lowering herself into a black stretch limo. 'Hey, Frank, we shopped, we ate. Take me home, baby.'

'Hey, Rick,' I whisper. 'Take me home, baby.'

He smiles and holds my hand and we walk down the road, everything temporarily forgotten, smoothed out and put away.

In the hotel we can do what we want, no dead parents on the mantelpiece, no unsold merchandise in the hall, no bills, no recorded delivery. We take off our clothes and climb into bed, switch on the telly, lie back on the stiff white pillows and kiss. The bed is solid and silent.

Afterwards I say, 'That was the best sex I've ever had.'

It wasn't. I just said it because I wanted it to be. He doesn't believe me, though it was good. He flicks the remote, channel-hopping. I'm almost asleep. Suddenly he drops the remote on the floor, rolls over and wraps himself round me, his cheek rough against the nape of my neck, his hand on my breast.

'It won't always be like this,' he says.

'I know.'

Some time in the small hours I wake. Rick is standing by the bare window, looking out. There ought to be moonlight, but the light changes colours: neon pink, orange, green. He's naked and I prop myself up on one elbow and prise my eyes open.

'What is it?'

He doesn't answer, only pulls the curtain shut.

'Rick?'

'On the subway –' he says. 'Woke up just now and remembered a bloke on the subway –' I can only just make him out. He's picked up his jacket and he holds it for a moment like a mother with a dead baby, then throws it at me. 'Bastard's lifted my fucking wallet,' he says. 'Cleaned us right out.'

I sit up and go through the pockets. He's having a nightmare: this is not really happening. Now I'm in the nightmare. *Il Patrone* is in the room, and Maria. His face is lugubrious but hers is downright malicious. He takes her in his arms and they waltz round the room. 'Are the luckiest people in the world,' they sing.

Picking up my pillow, I bury myself beneath it, but their voices come through. From now on, every pillow I sleep on will have them inside, mashed into the feathers like dust mites, a chorus in my ear.

I sit up again, swing my legs off the bed and go over to the window, throw the curtain wide. Now there is moonlight, high above the towers, a thin crescent moon. Rick's face is pallid. I grab his hand, half expect it to be cold.

'We can't let them win.'

'No?' he says.

'We still have our passports, our tickets.'

'Don't –'

'Don't what?'

'Don't say, And we still have each other.'

I let his hand drop and he turns and looks out of the window. The middle of the night and fourteen floors below there are people and cars. There is no night, only dark round the edges.

AMANDA WHITE

Granny's
blue-poodle period

I thought of Picasso
at her bedside or
taking a walk into the lounge
where faces hung in still-life lines
gone quietly wonky in front of the
giant-size telly
spewing out daytime obscenities
a view on the real world
they had all left behind
accelerating fast on wheelchairs
pooing in their pants
down the icy floors
through the floppy
old vagina flaps of doors
into the geriatric ward.

Granny had Parkinson's
sat in her pink blanket bed
insulting Albert her husband
swearing he was a homosexual
sure the Brazilian ancillary was
doing experiments with her wee
and I tried to retrieve some memory
that clear sight
before it got so bad
my little hand in hers
striding by the sea
her pointing out white horses
and the cross-Channel ferry
instead of blue poodles
curled around her swollen feet.

We took it in shifts to visit and sit
with flowers by the living grave-side
and on good days she sat up
looked out with her bright blue eyes
and made a stab at recognition
before collapsing into that
jigsaw of unmatching pieces
strangers by her bed
pretending to be relatives
our features in the wrong place
and once I imagined
I saw those blue poodles
even heard their barking
and they were smiling up at me
and wagging their tails.

The giraffe house

Untroubled by good or bad reviews
the giraffes sleep much of the time
when they're not snacking or just
hanging about on awkward corners.
They don't mind staying in, blinking
out at nothing in particular, that
other life they have only heard about,
passing by, there below, somehow hard
to focus on from such a height – not
unlike their neighbours of the short,
unpatterned and human kind, who
also live in captivity and zone one.

The stay

In your house not my house but welcoming
in my room once your room, spare and shifting
strange time now clocking a rip of afternoon
you downstairs preparing the carrots for death
and you had said stay as long as you like
but I saw the hard cash-balance of friendship
crack between the harsh laughter lines of your eyes
that pleasant offer to bring my friends over any time
and yet my stealing footsteps as I go to the toilet at night
having rehearsed every creak of landing
and held sheets around me for soundproofing
now I find myself announced into each room
eyed up suspiciously by possessions
fearful of inanimate objects going missing
that most precious of ornaments suddenly breaking
and the excuse of your words making light of accidents
as you frisk me for insurance policies.

I make friends with your bathroom and unfamiliar
brands of cosmetics, rape a blusher without touching
lock the door on this room for my leasing
with a mirror to guide fresh sight on features
and a place to hang my towel cousined close to yours
I take stock of belongings in new corners
the wait for where to make mess but not quite sure
the folded remnants of my life stillborn in boxes

with a view to the garden where idle birds whimper
getting used to the way the sash falls if opened
and the change in the temperature with each
flick of heating knowing when to switch on
and off again the hot water guilty of overindulgence
while I steal a drop of bubble bath and listen
to your movements in the kitchen beneath me
waiting for a sudden noise to give away my bearings
as you shout upstairs I am welcome to join you for dinner.

Rests in the music

Four Four. Common Time. Four crotchets or the same value in longer or short notes or rests and four have to be counted in a bar.

1 2 3 4   This is it, mostly, before and after acts of doing,

2 2 3 4   waiting rooms, queues, nothing special afternoons,

3 2 3 4   watching rain making out on windows,

4 2 3 4   playing patterns from curtains and shadows,

5 2 3 4   rolling a bogie in your fingers then eating it,

6 2 3 4   not the events that can be told properly,

7 2 3 4   when you ask me to tell you about my life,

8 2 3 4   but the uninteresting parts for those like me who aren't famous,

9 2 3 4   the jokes I can only half remember or

10 2 3 4   the days-in doing nothing that sandwich days-out

11 2 3 4   the ones we focus upon that show a successful equation,

12 2 3 4   a point worth making about why I'm here

13 2 3 4   and what I've done that really matters.

14 2 3 4   Painful then when these are forgotten or grow hazy by the onslaught

15 2 3 4   of the just being here days, the rests in the music, hummings,

16 2 3 4   the passing of seconds, naked heartbeats,

17 2 3 4   failed by all words and all languages spoken or otherwise,

18 2   3   4   nightmares for biographers of any species.

19 2   3   4   I am often jolted awake by small details
                 groping for attention,

20 2   3   4   dreams really are the worst filing cabinets,
                 meticulously indexing,

21 2   3   4   this is where the grommets of life lie,

22 2   3   4   sneaking around in the dull rooms of a brain,

23 2   3   4   that extra space scientists are still trying to
                 find,

24 2   3   4   but perhaps shouldn't bother about, because

25 2   3   4   it's there that these amoeba memoirs are,

26 2   3   4   taking the piss, lost neighbours and near
                 strangers perhaps seen once

27 2   3   4   mixed up with the real friends and family you
                 do see and can

28 2   3   4   string together in a well-constructed sentence
                 of cause and effect.

29 2   3   4   Mostly, I'm just counting out the time after
                 something happened

30 2   3   4   and before something else will happen again,
                 like falling in love or nearly dying,
                 those cymbal crashes we can talk about,

1   2   3   4   unlike the rest of it that leaves you there
                 amongst the crowds

2   2   3   4   cloud-watching and table-tapping,

3   2   3   4   the tiny dots of life hanging about on the
                 corners of insanity,

4   2   3   4   great gangs of futility beating up the little
                 specks of real activity,

5   2   3   4   perhaps that's why some take to murder and
                 smaller crimes,

6 2 3 4   just to get out from under the pressure of
            empty pages in diaries,
7 2 3 4   the dead-leg hours of being bored and aimless
8 2 3 4   that make talk of evolution and progress
            ridiculous,
9 2 3 4   when mostly, we're still playing monkeys,
10 2 3 4   picking scabs and foldings and washings and
            body functions,
11 2 3 4   visiting the toilet more often than other
            countries and
12 2 3 4   places we might have circled on maps
13 2 3 4   that try to interrupt this countdown to death.
14 2 3 4

STEPHANIE HALE

Firebug

It is said of Norfolk that the land is so flat, so relentlessly and unremittingly flat, that it can send people mad. That seeing such vast distances so devoid of character or feature – except perhaps for the occasional twisted willow – does something peculiar to the mind. There are many disbelievers in this theory; especially amongst those whose bloodlines are tied to the land, those whose families have lived and bred here for generations.

Eva Burnett was a believer. She had no doubts at all about the validity of this theory.

There is a certain stretch between Norwich and the coastline where there seems to be nothing between oneself and the sea but miles and miles of nothingness. No cows, no sheep, no scarecrows, no outhouses, no sheds, no homes, no people. Only the occasional mound of brown sugar beet piled high in the fields for collection.

Here, Eva thought, one could truly understand what it was like to be mad. To be so utterly devoid of stimulation that the brain turned inside out with frustration.

The sky was bigger in Norfolk. Infinitely, infinitely bigger. In the day, the quality of the light was different. Flat and uniform and unflinching. There was no escape from the light, even in the shadows. It was at night, though, that the sky excelled itself. At certain times of the year, the sky was like a mirror which magnified the light of the planets and made them glow orange. The moon shone not white, but gold, blazing like a giant ball of fire. There was little that could rival a Norfolk moon.

Eva Burnett worked in the White Hotel just off the coastal road leading from Cromer to Hunstanton. It was a flat plain stretch frequented by swans and white geese. Feathers blew over the road as often as leaves. Though seagulls sometimes soared on the air currents, they were mute. Their hungry yelps were lost in the gusts of wind.

In truth, Eva was fortunate to have the position. The hotel manager, Clarissa Pinfield, had been persuaded to take her on by the director of a children's home in Overstrand. 'I'm not denying that she's a bit odd,' he'd said. 'But give her a chance. Everyone deserves a chance.' Clarissa had owed him a favour and who, after all, could turn away a teenage orphan?

When Clarissa saw that the girl's long brown hair was neatly tied back in a ponytail (no noticeable dandruff, no noticeable knots), that she wore flat shoes, tan-coloured nylons and a sensible skirt, she was relieved.

The unease only came later. Later, when she noticed that the girl's hairless skin reminded her of a suckling pig. Later, when she noticed that her eyes were pale and unrimmed. For when

Eva smiled, her eyes did not crease up like neat black starfish. Instead, her face looked as featureless and bland as a portrait by Matisse. She had no eyebrows either, nothing by which to judge her thoughts or feelings. Her neatly combed hair was, in fact, a wig. The girl was quite hairless.

Only later did Mrs Pinfield discover this – otherwise, she swore, she would never have given the wretched girl the job.

Nor was this all. Worse, much worse than any of this, was the final discovery: Eva Burnett had neither palms nor finger-prints.

It did not matter whether Eva was awake or asleep when the dreams came to her, whether her eyes were open or closed. For in her sleep and in her waking hours alike, she could sense the presence of her mother's spirit.

One morning, shortly towards the end of the breakfast shift, while she was still up to her elbows in slippery white bubbles of grease, Eva heard a muffled voice somewhere inside the kitchen.

'Eva! Eva!' The voice was so soft it might have been the wind whispering through the dangling leaves of a willow tree. So soft, it might have been the dying breath of a summer storm.

'Eeeva! Eeeeevaaaa!'

She ignored it and carried on scrubbing the frying pans. But no, there it was again.

'Let me out! Help me out of here!'

Eva put down her scourer and wiped off her arms with the raw edge of a tea-towel. 'Mum! Is that you?' She walked over to the cupboards where the knife blocks and chopping boards were kept.

'Open the door, will you? It's dark in here! And boiling hot too!' The voice was terse; already irritated.

And, though her mother was dead, long long dead, Eva answered. 'Where are you?'

'In here! Right in front of you!'

'Wait for the chef to leave and I'll let you out!'

'No! N*ow*!'

Seeing herself alone in the kitchen, Eva opened the doors of all the cupboards at chest and knee height. Bang! Bang! Bang! Bang! Bang! Bang! She pulled out all the metal saucepans, stacked inside one another like Russian dolls. She looked inside them, separating mother from daughter so that the white stone tiles were covered with cauldrons and frying pans and milk pans. When she had done this, she pulled the metal lids out of the cupboards and let these too clatter on the cold floor. Her mother's ghost was not in any of the normal hiding places.

'Stop playing games, will you? I've got work to do!'

'You're not looking hard enough. You don't want to find me! Hurry up! I'm running out of air!' Her mother was wheezing, her breath as high and sharp as a tin whistle.

'Hang on! Wait a minute! I'll find you!'

With an infuriating, but growing sense of urgency, she found herself tugging at the cutlery drawers, pulling so hard that they flew off their plastic rails; rummaging through the contents, through wooden spoons, ladles, whisks, fruit peelers, potato mashers; finally, in desperation, checking the knife block, pulling the knives one by one onto the Formica surface: the carving knife, the bread knife, the grapefruit knife, the peeler, the boning knife. Still no sign of her mother.

'Are you all right? Can you hold on?'

'Don't worry about me, dear. I'll be all right.' Yet she could hear the asthmatic wheezing, the way her mother's chest heaved as if it was sucking in treacle.

'Just stay calm.' Trying to stay calm herself, but panicking.

'I'm all right, dear. Really, I am.'

But coughing. Gasping. Wheezing. Then silence. And in this silence, frantically tugging open the door of the oven. And seeing, halfway down, a roast pork and cider pie. Along the edges where the pastry met the plate, a pair of pale lips with a tiny brown tongue.

Burning her fingers, she pulled the plate out without the oven gloves, almost dropping it in the process. The pie was panting slightly, but it was alive.

'Mum!' Incredulous. Her mother as a piece of shortcrust pastry.

'You took your time. I'd almost given up hope.'

'What are you doing here? *And why do you look like that?*'

Her mother, as she usually did, ignored the question. 'Nice way to greet your mother! Aren't you going to give me a kiss?'

Kissing the pie on its floury brown cheek. Blistering her lips. Feeling ridiculous. 'You've got to stop doing this!'

'Why? I like to keep an eye on you. Make sure you're being looked after.'

'I'm fine.'

'You should be working in an office. Not a kitchen. With your qualifications.'

'What qualifications?'

'Working in a kitchen as a skivvy! You should never have let them talk you into it.'

'I don't mind.'

'They're walking all over you. Taking advantage.'

And in that same horrible moment, Eva heard another voice behind her. This time, deeper and male.

Realising it to be the chef who was staring, disbelieving, at the pans scattered on the floor, at the silver glitter of unsheathed blades. Tucking the meat pie into the front pocket of her uniform. Then running as fast as she could to the staff toilets and locking the door. Trying as hard as she might to coax the pie to speak again. Taking it back to the children's home with her, and watching it slowly rot, the pastry turning first black, then powdery green.

Looking out on the Norfolk sky and wondering if the dreams would ever end. If the smell of rotting meat would ever go away.

Silence, then, for another month.

The chef was kindly and forgiving, fond of Eva in a fatherly sort of way. Remembered reports of the house fire in the *Eastern Daily Press*. Felt for the girl. Unable to imagine losing an entire family in flames. Had daughters of his own. Knew they acted damn peculiar even with their parents still alive. Forgave his kitchen hand on condition that she promise to eat properly and at proper times if she was hungry; and never to do the same thing again.

Clarissa Pinfield, on the other hand, was less forgiving. She did not know about the meat pie incident. Her dislike was rooted in more fertile ground.

Some people are indelibly marked by life and never learn to mask the tragedy in their eyes. They are easy prey for pack-leaders who despise runts and weaklings. Eva Burnett was such a girl. Clarissa tried to feel pity, but instead was filled with an irrational animal hatred. Though she loathed herself for loathing the girl, she never quite overcame the feeling. Angry because the unease was self-inflicted: it had been she who'd employed the orphan in the first place. 'I'll watch her closely,' she promised herself. 'One false move, just one, and she's out!'

Then, one lunchtime –

Screaming. A shrill voice trilling obscenities, singing abuse not fit for human ears.

'Eedjut! Eedjuuut!'

There could be no doubt where the ghost was hiding. The grill was ablaze, flames licking the painted metal. Eva leapt to her feet and snatched the tray out of the fire. Damping down the flames with a tea-towel.

'Moron! Idiot!'

The lamb cutlets were charred at the edges. The fat curling up like shrivelled slugs.

'The number of times you've been told *not to turn your back on the grill*! And do you listen? Look what happens *when you don't listen.*'

Tears in Eva's throat suddenly. Choking on her answer. Spitting grief and saliva. 'I don't know how to. I've never been taught.'

'Learn then! *Pay attention!*'

The chef had been stirring a peppercorn and rosemary sauce. But now the whirring of the grinder stopped and he came to turn the meat. Prongs in hand, he snapped at the air like a crab, waving the pincers comically as if he would pinch any member of staff who happened to be in his way. Eva did not respond as he had hoped. Instead, she snatched the cutlet away and could not be persuaded to give it back.

'Well, I'll be damned!' the chef said. 'If you want it that bad, then you'd better have it. If you're hungry, you only have to ask. We're not short of food around here.' He disappeared and returned with a plate of chips. Then he made Eva sit down to eat them. Fond as he was of her, he could sense the situation was starting to get out of hand.

Eva Burnett had been working at the White Hotel for less than twelve weeks when she was summoned to Clarissa Pinfield's office. Her probationary period was drawing to an end.

'I understand you're settling in well,' Clarissa said. Her lips curled like a snarling dog's. Furious at the girl. In three months, she had earned a reputation for being both obedient and industrious. There had been rumours, as yet unsubstantiated, of Eva stealing food. Otherwise, nothing suspicious.

'The chef's given you a glowing reference. He wants me to upgrade you and put you on day release.' Clarissa looked at the arch where Eva's eyebrows should have been; at her unblinking fish-like eyes. She could not tell whether she was pleased or displeased; even whether she was listening. 'It will mean attending college once a week. And of course, a small pay rise.'

The girl's face was like a blank white page waiting to be written upon. Like a meadow of unsullied snow, waiting for muddying footsteps. Spineless, Clarissa thought, utterly spineless. She noticed that the girl's wig had slipped back slightly to reveal a slope of shiny pink skin. She felt a slight wave of nausea. This is the limit! she thought. The absolute limit. Next thing, she'll be strutting around without her uniform. Or worse still, coming into work bald! Something has to be done about this. She has to be told.

She smiled across her desk at Eva, a forced grin which revealed the blunt line of her teeth. Then she leaned on her elbows, unintentionally wafting the air, so that suddenly Eva could smell the cinnamon of her skin.

'One other thing, as one woman to another.' Clarissa's voice was sweet as a meringue. 'Perhaps you could sort out the problem with your hair. Maybe buy some false lashes? Or pencil in some eyebrows? I wouldn't want you to feel uncomfortable around the other staff.'

She shook the girl's hand firmly to signal the end of the interview. Then shuddered as she looked down. This was the first time she realised that Eva had no palms or fingerprints.

So Eva was promoted from kitchen hand to staff trainee. She moved out of the children's home and into her own room at the White Hotel. But the dreams continued.

One morning, her mother appeared to her in the bottom of a big silver frying pan. She had tipped the fat down the plughole, when a cluster of bacon bits sticking to the bottom started to move.

'I hope you're not going to wash me!'

'For God's sake! You made me jump!' Looking down, exasperated, into the scratched metal and seeing her own face reflected back like a ghost. 'Of course I'm washing the pan.'

'Don't you worry about that chef. You leave him to me!'

'Please, I like this job. Don't spoil things for me.'

'So you'd drown your own mother just to save your own skin?'

'It's not like that.'

'The pan's hardly been used. No one will notice.'

'I'll compromise, then. I'll leave it until last.'

So she washed up everything else. The grapefruit glasses first of all. Next, the side plates smeared with crumbs and marmalade. After this, the breakfast plates, slippery with sausage grease and bacon rind. She used the brush to scrub away the dried egg and tomato ketchup from the cutlery. Finally, she washed the saucepans used to boil the tomatoes and tinned mushrooms.

Only the giant frying pan was left. 'Your turn now.'

'I forbid you to do it.'

'It'll only take a second. Just hold your breath. You'll be all right.'

'I won't! You're trying to kill me!'

'You're already dead!' Eva, becoming frustrated now, already working over her shift. Putting the frying pan in the water so that air bubbles rushed to the surface. Swilling the frying pan as quickly as she could. Dipping it in and out to allow her mother time to take air.

Behind her, the chef was ready to leave. He had discarded his whites for a leather jacket, and was jangling a bunch of keys. A motorcycle helmet looped over his arm. 'Stop faffing about!' he said cheerfully. 'Let me do it! Give it a good swilling! Like this!' Dunking the frying pan into the water himself. Scrubbing it hard with a scourer. 'Bit of elbow grease.' He grinned. 'Is all that's needed.' Then, having washed out the bacon bits, he put on his helmet. 'See you tomorrow,' he said cheerily, and left.

'Mum! Mum! Are you still there?'

No sign of her. Only a faint voice, coming from the kitchen sink. 'How could you? My own daughter! My own flesh and blood!'

'It was the chef. Not me.'

'You should be ashamed of yourself! Killing your own
mother!'

Eva, at staff breakfast, watching Clarissa Pinfield about to sink
her teeth into a steak sandwich. Her staring face all the more
disturbing with its new kohl eyebrows and nylon eyelashes.
Seeing the repulsion in Clarissa's eyes. Then watching with
horror as the bread crusts parted like lips, the sliver of flash-fry
steak curling like a tongue in between.

'Get me out of here! Don't let this bitch eat me.'

Clarissa, lifting the sandwich to her lips. Nearer and nearer
to those blunt teeth. The air strong with the scent of cinnamon.

'*Do something*! Don't just sit there! *Get off your arse and do
something*!'

Eva poised like a hungry panther. Leaping to the sandwich.
Snatching it from her manager's hand. Hearing in that same
instant the triumphant shout of a tired hunter. The flash of joy
in Clarissa's eyes. Thinking: This is it. I am in trouble now. I am
going to lose my job.

Clarissa staring back with the cold confidence of a woman
holding a loaded rifle. Saying calmly: 'Perhaps you'd like to
step into my office, Eva.'

Feeling the air bristle. Overpowered by the scent of sweet
spice. Looking out on the Norfolk sky, and knowing something
important and big is about to happen.

'I know you've been having problems settling in.'

Eva hardly hearing the words, knowing what was coming.
Listening unnecessary, a mere formality.

'To lose one's family is a terrible thing. But while I sympath-
ise, that's no excuse for –' Noticing as she talked, a movement
in her hand. The steak sandwich struggling to speak. Straining

her ears. The bread compressed and squashing the meat so it could hardly move. 'And we do pride ourselves on a certain reputation.' Eyes darting about the office. Coming to rest on a pile of spiked papers. Shifting to a bowl of matches, each packet embossed with the hotel's coat of arms. After this, glancing at the expensive oak panelling which lined the walls.

The ghost finding its voice. More distinctive now. This time, the words emanating not from the sandwich, but from inside Eva's head.

'I'm afraid we're going to have to let you go, though you will be allowed to –'

Beyond Clarissa's shoulder, the window. Outside, an exposed landscape and an unshielded sky. Eva felt as though her whole life had been building to this single moment. That she had been born to carry out this solitary act.

The forecast was for hard frost and a clear uncloudy night. The stars would be out and the Norfolk sky would set the planets aflame. At midnight, the White Hotel would be a brilliant ball of fire. The wild glitter on earth would rival that of the moon.

WENDY RICHMOND

Two cats and a desk in the kitchen

That first evening she gave me the family bit, solid, I thought,
        very grounded, her with her razzmatazz life, sending out
because she never learnt to cook, two jobs, a night life worth
                                                                envy
        and regular four-hour spins to hit the weekend surf.
I declined to see the sights, knew I had to get stuck in
        knuckle down and produce enough before going back
to children, soaps and the local on Wednesdays.
        She goes, hair free to the wind, long mac flapping
as she faces it full. I hadn't grasped the lengths to which she
                                                                needed
        to seem healthy, strong, weighted as she was.
I liked the way she didn't once refer to her figure, or let an
                                                                inch pass
        before moving on to discuss subjects that suited.

I watch from the window, then warm my back against the
                                                    radiator.
      When I first got ill she was all confession, a sickly child,
her mother vengeful from lounge to kitchen how kids ruin
                                                    your life.
      Saw then how she clasped her hands, clicked her
                                                    thumbnails,
the even smile, and the way she so very carefully paced her
                                                    steps
      and how once, just once, dropped her knife when I
                                                    joked
about training the kids for my dotage. And I understood why
      she couldn't ever spend a life with mirrors, domesticity
and the shadows of the cage of a singular place she never
                                                    much lived in
      a flat with two cats and a desk in the kitchen.

The day job

Sheer hell. Forgot to charge the mobile overnight,
then couldn't find client's file, so made it up
on the spot, let him do most of the talking.

Assured him baked beans are still good, steady
like a tree growing out of rock. Perpetual
like the rain in Seattle.

Got carried away with metaphor, but impressed
I think. Was it twenty-six or eighteen shares he wanted
to invest? Memory is so hazy of late.

Still, doesn't make many odds, will stick it all
in Whale Preservation anyway. Stuff baked beans.

Father called, wants to meet up, talk about childhood,
Mother, something about sucking dummies.

The way of it

Sometimes there's a sax sweating of the earth mined jewel,
and the men herded to labour for the sparkle.
But our land has brass bands trumpeting the end
of a pit, the coal-dust settling into the mud.

    My sister writes to me of home
    where the fields sag over the seams,
    gutting the ground, like a mattress.

Sometimes there's a coil of white cloud pulling my eyes
off the gutter and into just blue.

    My sister asks for a reply
    repeating that He will forgive
    all again and again, and more.

Sometimes it's the way the blade of the knife gorges
out the potato's eye, slices the chips in the palm.

    My sister tells of a mother's apron,
    the way of the wiping of her hands.
    She has stopped dyeing her hair.

Sometimes it's a knitting pattern, red polo-neck
with large snowflakes, sometimes a painted metal bucket
and books always books and the red lipstick.
Most times it's the sweat of the sax.

CANDY NEUBERT

Clear mirror,
quiet water

The best kind of client is the one who does not talk much. Any
stylist will tell you so, anyone who has cut hair for more than,
say, a year. It is not the hair-cutting which gets tiresome – it
takes time for an artist to tire of his art – it is the conversations
we are forced into at the same time.

Mrs Beecham is one of the best. Shoulder-length mousy
bob, trimmed four times a year with wash and blow-dry.
Pleasant smile, same as usual, thank you so much, and a small
tip in the box.

I don't judge my clients by the size of their tips (though nat-
urally I notice the generous ones). No, I appreciate the
tranquillity of a wet head of hair, tilted this way and that to my
fingers, and uninterrupted by talk. This is how I do my best
work. I see the head, shaped and made beautiful by the softness of hair – for what would we be without it, but skulls? I see
it, feel it, persuade it into beauty; the act is a whole one. I am

interested in Zen, yes. I always give Mrs Beecham a perfect cut.

Will she come back again after today?

A client once came into the South Molton Street salon with that same brown, straight hair. The stylist – what was his name? – ran his comb through it and suggested a light perm. She seemed surprised. No, she just wanted a trim, a good one. He lifted a few strands and went on to suggest some colouring, perhaps highlights.

How insensitive! How offensive! And certainly she seemed offended, but politely murmured that she liked her own hair colour.

'Oh, Plain Jane!' he said.

Unforgivable, of course. He forgot himself, in my opinion. Or thought himself too expensive to care. Anyhow, the woman walked out of the salon exactly as she was, with her wet hair and one of our olive-green towels still around her shoulders. Madam, I applaud you to this day.

This was the moment, I believe, when the crassness of London became clear to me; when I decided to pursue my art in a place of decorum and good manners.

Hereford. Hair Design by Arthur, Hereford. I beg you to pro-nounce 'Arthur' correctly, even in your mind. I remember Marilyn (Reception) used the soft English 'th' when she came to be interviewed, but now to clients she is at pains – is that the idiom? – to stress the hard 't' as we do in Switzerland. Like so: R Tour.

Arthur and I are the only Swiss in Hereford, I'm fairly sure. And in Hereford, I have only cut the hair of women. My lover

Rodney has mixed feelings about this. Every day I touch only women: six, eight, sometimes as many as ten.

Men are more fearful. The very word in English: 'hairdresser'! They do not want their hair dressed. They hardly want it cut, hardly care to admit that it even grows. In London, it was different: all sorts of men, but – crass. In country towns like Hereford the men do not enter salons of hair design.

Once, just once, a gentleman came in as if by mistake. He blinked his eyes, trying to assess his surroundings, and Arthur hurried him into a seat (we were quiet that afternoon) to give him a cut in a very tasteful, understated style. Perhaps the man was travelling through this part of the country, but anyway we have not seen him again. You can pick up a great deal through the tips of the fingers, and likewise through the scalp from someone else's fingertips. Perhaps that is what put him off.

I left London after my first true glimpse of English spirit. Did the woman with the wet hair throw the towel aside or fold it neatly into her bag? Did she let it remain on her shoulders, tossing her head on her way down Bond Street?

Aside from this woman, the English people have no *élan*. No *élan*, but heart. They are weighed down by heart. See the way Marilyn sits at her desk, and how Jackie moves the broom between the chairs: faultless, but heavy. Also Mrs Cunningham on a Friday, her husband reading a newspaper in the car outside, and indeed all of Hereford passing by. The body language has a look of – what is the word? Viscose? Maybe that is not right; I have a shirt made of viscose. But you have the right word already: heavy-hearted. That is it. We do not walk like that in the streets of Lausanne.

It was Mrs Beecham today who opened my eyes. Today I

was moved by a woman in a way I would never have thought possible.

Shall I tell Rodney? If I do, then it must be this very evening, or not at all, for it would seem odd to simply mention such a thing casually in the future. The subject of women is not an easy one for Rodney. It is enough that I treat them with care and tenderness every day. This is important.

Arthur has done much to enhance my skill, and he taught me two things. Firstly, to talk with the outer edge of one's soul. To know that this edge is vast and infinite and so it is possible to remember, without detracting from one's work, that Mrs Elliot has a daughter at boarding-school, that Miss Neave breeds Dobermann pinschers, and so on. They come for this, this contact of words. Secondly, the physical care, the sure touch. It is a form of love. Which leads me back to Mrs Beecham.

She sat before the mirror this afternoon in a blue robe such as each client wears. She nodded hello, fell into her usual silence, and I began. The hair is divided into sections – I use only one clip – and the cut begins at the nape of the neck, that exquisite place. In most cases the client instinctively inclines forward, an attitude of submission. I find this touching. Thus we give assent to the will of others, to love, to execution. I think of these things and my thoughts flow into my hands. This is why it is harder when the flow is broken by conversation, but the true master will not notice this. Arthur, for example.

I cut the hair at the back, section by section to the crown. The left side, and the right. I lift the hair from the scalp with unvarying tension. Some clients, even when silent, make jerking movements as they reach for coffee cups or turn pages. But a few, like Mrs Beecham, close their eyes and are perfectly still. Not even tempted by the mirror! To concentrate one's mind, as the Japanese say: clear mirror, quiet water. Lovely, is it not? And the English: still waters run deep. How the cultural differences echo through the two phrases! So two beings, foreign to one another, are concentrated, artist and living subject, linked by a fingerful of hair.

Rodney teases me about my lyricism. 'Over the top,' as he puts it. Rodney's own idea of romance is obtuse (I have just referred to the dictionary for 'obtuse' and I believe this to be my meaning). He has attractive blunt hands, also. But no *élan*! No, I shall not recount Mrs Beecham's haircut to Rodney.

Thus because of a second English woman I shall move again, this time back to Switzerland. Not immediately, but soon enough. For I realise that if I cannot share Mrs Beecham with Rodney, with whom can I share any of my innermost thoughts?

She was acutely aware of my touch; of course I sensed this. But only when I came to check the length of the hair in front of her face, bending towards her, did I realise that she was in more than a state of trance, that with her hand beneath the robe she was, in fact, pleasuring herself. How else can I say it? And like a lover driven to accompany his love along the meandering path towards joy, I continued to cut. Combing across her head, lifting the hair, pulling it gently away from the scalp, and – snip snip – back to the nape of the neck (she exhaled in a tiny sigh) and up to the crown, left side and right side again.

A quick glance in the mirror assured me that we were unobserved. Arthur was discussing something with a new client, Marilyn talking into the telephone, and our trainee out of sight with Jackie in the back room.

I returned with awe to the experience before me, in my very hands. I ran the edge of the comb behind the ears, coaxed the hair between my fingers. My scissors sang with their own music. I thought: I am as close to a woman as I will ever be. With total wonder, I heard her small cry and glanced quickly again into the mirror. Arthur still spoke to his client, Marilyn into the telephone; cups and saucers clattered from the back. A tear came from beneath Mrs Beecham's closed lids and ran down her cheek.

I had noticed nothing, had I? I knew nothing. I reached for the drier, feeling, for once, clumsy. But then her eyes opened and she smiled in her pleasant, distant way.

'Don't bother drying it,' she said.

She paid, and left a small tip. Out into the world, another woman tossing her wet hair, as she will do so for ever on the pavements of memory. Cut a little shorter, perhaps, than usual.

JADWIGA BILLEWICZ

Colouring the shadows

I know yellow. It is
the velvet pile of snapdragons, a purse
to slip your fingers into. Not foxgloves.

Mimosa, a cat I had once,
was a yellow cat. She purred
like butter, stirred the sun on the porch
with busy claws, watched the hay-making
with slanted eyes.

I will wear yellow. Slide silk on silk
on thighs, smooth out my stockings, tuck
arthritic fingers into buttonholes like Braille.

Not foxgloves. Do not give me purple

it crushes my chest.

Scar tissue

This morning I list their expenses; the three of them
elbow-deep in dishes singing each in a different off-key key
partly remembered words from way way somewhere
where they meet still, now, beneath the singing
in black bread and sour potato wine. Enough

to make the dog howl for those wild Siberian winds
that cut you raw and ragged until your lungs grate
with dust even at this Northumbrian sink, even now,
with the sun furrowing their wrinkled smiles. It was

a land for giants. You know this for quite certain
as certain as the picture of a cow on the cream fudge
your aunt brings when she visits, as clear
as the heavy veining on her hands, robust and frail
like the ribs of cabbage leaves. And you try

to imagine with your skin the taste of mine-shafts
but the nearest you can get is Nenthead
and the hope of garnet in a worked-out lead seam you once
went into for a whole hundred yards without a torch.

The grazes on my hands are local sandstone.

Home

It's only cardboard
but somehow
never the right
size and it's hard
to get the corners
sharp when you score
the edges for
cutting down.
Then it won't
lie straight; and
the edges overlap.

You can't see,
but it's cosy, here
with the sides so close,
raising the fine hairs
on the back of
my hand. Paper
caress stroking
my neck, tucking
my knees all the way
up to my chin.

My breathing
creeps round
to the soles
of my feet.

Icicle chains

We have winters here. The snow is not
Deep. The wind
Is cut with salt. I'd never seen the sea
Then
We skated on thick ice. Rolled
Soft in drifts I was warm
With brothers
Then
Not here.

We have garlands here. Draperies breathless
With colour
Freeze the air. I'd never seen the North
Then
We inhaled orchards. Gathering
Fragrant juices I was warm
With brothers
Then
Not here.

ANNE SUMMERFIELD

The nerve

Sometimes people come up to him in bars or family restaurants and say 'Weren't you Somebody once?' and then they buy
him beers or meals or have an aunt who does rooms for the
night. Once we got a whole tank full of gas from a red-haired
guy who'd courted his wife in front of *Cowboy Corral*. We drove
away waving and smiling like minor English royalty.

'I don't recall being in that movie,' he said a mile further
down the road. 'It was probably Redford, but what the hell.'

When we first met I was just like everyone else: thought I
recalled the raise of a brow or the twitch of a lip. And I remembered a wet afternoon in a seaside cinema, gazing at that giant
Technicolor face on the screen, fragile and iridescent as the surface of a bubble. But I said nothing. Just got him his tuna melt
on rye and black coffee, just talked about the heat and whether
cream or ice-cream went best with apple pie. And all the time
I'm wearing my cherry-coloured uniform with the too-short skirt
and he's trying to look at my arse – he's none too subtle about

it either – and I'm thinking: It must be him, it's got to be him.

Next day we go on the road.

He lives nowhere. At first I assume it's research, just temporary for him, this constant shifting from one dirt-track town to another. But we travel on and on: a night here, a day there. Sometimes I feel like I'm on a ride in an amusement park – you know the ones – where the car stays still and they just show the scenery moving around you. I feel like we could just ask the projectionist to switch off and we'd be sitting in some old movie lot surrounded by crumbling plywood sets and the left-over bicycle from *Butch Cassidy*. But sometimes, most times, I forget that there could be anything different.

When I first came to America (O, land of dreams; O, land paved with gold) I wanted it all. I wanted to pose in shorts on the Hollywood sign, one leg casually swung over the second 'O'. I wanted to whoosh down white-water rapids in a bright yellow inflatable, wrestle with wild brown bears in Yellowstone, touch the stony noses of giant presidents, drive across the Grand Canyon in my scarlet convertible, climb the Empire State Building on the outside. I would eat breakfast at Tiffany's. And one day, yes, I would be famous. I would be Somebody. In the land of plenty it would all be easy, surely. All I needed was the nerve.

The nerve got me on the plane in the grey rain of Gatwick and landed me safe in the hot smoke of LA. The nerve got me on a Greyhound to the waitressing job a friend of a friend claimed was there for the taking. The nerve then mysteriously packed up and left me serving fries in the Midwest. I figured that going with him was a way of getting even.

*

He never talks much about his past and I don't ask. One night we drive by a movie theatre as bright as Christmas lights, and I make some joke about going back to catch the show, and he looks at me as if I'm crazy. The other dude ranchers who made good in *Cowboy Corral* are still there: directing, or making guest appearances on the *Tonight* show. And he's here, on the road, running to or from.

He always introduces me just by name. 'This is Shona,' he says and it is up to them to work out if I am wife, friend, lover or daughter. Mostly they get it right. He never needs to say who he is. People know.

We always stay in small towns, sometimes making wide sweeping detours to skim round cities. We avoid tourist places, any national monuments or parks, anywhere with the faintest whiff of fame. And so, as I zigzag across my adopted land, I see nothing more educational than Dunkin Donuts on a workday morning, nothing more startling than the scarlet roof of a Pizza Hut set against a clouded sky. He always needs to be the brightest star.

Today we are travelling another road to nowhere when the signs begin.

FREE WATER. The sign is hand-painted, peeling a little at one corner. ONLY A HUNDRED MILES TO GO.

The next sign is maybe five miles further on: FREE COFFEE AND DONUTS FOR HONEYMOONERS. I glance across and wonder if it's worth pretending.

VISIT THE WORLD-FAMOUS DRUG STORE!

We start to count the signs. When we reach fifty he gets bored, but I carry on silently. As we get nearer they are planted thicker on the ground until there is barely time to read one before the next appears. Enticing, tempting, seducing, mocking.

DON'T BE THE ONLY ONE WHO HAS NEVER BEEN!

'Can we go there?' I rarely ask him for anything; I rarely need to. 'Just for a little while?' He gives me a sideways look and continues driving.

The sun makes the asphalt glimmer and the glare makes me nauseous. The car we were loaned is only a Band C and the low roof makes me feel trapped in a cube of heat. 'I need the john,' I lie. 'They must have one with all that free coffee.'

We follow the signs and steer into a vast parking lot. There is an area set out for coaches and, as we drive past, a group of middle-aged tourists dressed in colours of the playroom are spilling out on to the tarmac with much tangling of camera straps and exaggerated laughter. A woman dressed in fluorescent orange sunglasses and Bermuda shorts printed with scarlet Scottie dogs attempts to descend the coach steps and is caught expertly by a balding man on the ground. 'Easy does it, Margy,' chorus the party, so loudly that it penetrates the car's interior. I stare straight ahead, pretending to look for a parking space.

We stop abruptly. I had expected him to stay in the car and wait for me, but he is the first out. As I close the car door, I glimpse something extremely tall and unnaturally green on the skyline. Focusing, I realise it is the neck of a dinosaur cowering behind the store.

He shambles inside, moving slowly through light and dark like a shadow puppet. I can see he's taking it all in, from the buffalo heads on the wall to the cookie counter painted like double choc chip and boasting 87 *Varieties Home Baked Fresh Each Morning*. He turns to look back at me and his smile is as honest as a child's.

'I'll meet you by the free coffee,' he says, and almost collides with a shop dummy dressed as Chief Sitting Bull. He laughs and I see, fleetingly, the handiwork of a leading Hollywood dentist.

When I return from the Ladies, he is telling stories in the Silver Dollar coffee bar, leaning his chair back against a life-size wood carving of the Sundance Kid. The customers and Sundance are equally silent and absorbed, so I go to look at Genuine Gemstone Jewelry and souvenir rattlesnake ashtrays. I wander through the leather-scented tack room and wonder who buys the gold-initialled bullwhips and what for. Then I listen to the animatronic cowboy orchestra play 'Home on the range' on fiddle, washboard and kazoo, and waste a dime having my fortune told by a talking parrot.

In time, I come into a backyard where the coach party are posing with Harvey the six-foot stuffed rabbit and noisily eating their honeymooners' donuts. There is little to buy in the yard, just candy canes and a few postcards on a single wall stand. But the coach party have found plenty of photo opportunities. As well as the rabbit, there's a chuck-wagon for happy hay rides, a three-foot-high Mount Rushmore, and a pink Cadillac without wheels. All of these are scrambled over and flashed at in turn with much high-pitched amusement.

In the one peaceful corner there is a mechanical bucking bronco, fifty cents a ride. The bronco is painted a greyish brown, and its mane and tail are matted black fluff, like a teddy bear that's been played with for too long. The saddle is a real one, with silver scrolls trimming its dark tooled leather. It is tied with cinches in front and behind the broad vertical drive-shaft, which both impales the beast and brings it to life. Around on the ground, dusty faded mattresses prepare to pad the inevitable fall. In front of the empty saddle a sign: *Ride the Bronco for three minutes. WIN A BIG PRIZE!*

As I stand staring, I hear the voices behind me and I become aware of the space closing as it fills with a warm tide of bodies. The coach party are swooping in on the bronco from all sides of the yard, abandoning Cadillac and rabbit alike. I try to escape and find myself trapped at nose-touching distance of Mount Rushmore.

'He's gonna ride the bronco,' hisses the balding man crushed next to me. 'Imagine, a big star like him, riding the Wall Drug bronco.'

'Get a shot of this, George,' barks the woman in sunglasses. The balding man is sweating, drops gathering on his forehead. 'Margy is just his biggest fan,' he apologises as he elbows out his camera.

Like well-trained extras, the crowd parts on cue to allow the talent to pass through. He waits beside the bronco, patting its plaster cheek just below the wild plaster eye. He has borrowed a ten-gallon hat, probably from a rich Texan running a side bet, and in it he looks younger and fresh. Everyone from the store, customers and staff alike, is crushed into the hot little yard before he swings his leg over the tattered bronco, eases himself into the saddle and gives the command for somebody's fifty cents to be put in the slot.

The bronco makes a curious whirring sound and doesn't seem set to move at all. Then suddenly it starts to judder and the precarious violent movements begin. The plaster body swirls and cavorts: not just up and down, but round and back, twirling and pirouetting, up and round, head down and then side to side. The hat lands in the dirt within seconds.

I can see from his face that it is harder than he'd expected. Some two-bit kids' ride, he must have thought. But no: rodeo stars train on these things and there he is, and I don't know if he's ever done his own stunts before, but this time he can't yell for a body double. The lines on his face go into sharp focus, and his eyes are as wild as the bronco's. His check shirt pleats across his back with the strain, bunches up under his arms and pulls taut across his chest. Each time he seems to have found the rhythm, the bronco changes, and they are locked in an insane dance, bounding from tempo to tempo, from quickstep to Charleston, via the funky chicken.

At first the crowd gasps and cheers as he survives each new twist and bounce. But they must see, as much as I do, how he is struggling, fighting. The balding man becomes so absorbed in watching that his camera remains frozen at nose height. Margy even removes her bright sunglasses so that she can observe more closely. There's a stillness, like dusts settling over the crowd.

At the moment when it seems things cannot get worse, he is tipped almost completely off a plaster shoulder and then backwards, legs clapping over the bronco's neck. In slow motion, I see him rise out of the saddle, forwards and down, and then grab at that silver pommel, heave himself impossibly back into his seat. The crowd lets out its breath with a joyous yahoo and, as the bronco halts, its three minutes spent, I see, perhaps everyone sees, a look I remember as he dismounts, satisfied, to retrieve the hat and take his bow with a sweep of the hand.

'Nearly thought ole Paint had me beat.'

And the crowd is laughing as well as clapping, yelling 'Ride him, cowboy' and I see him whooping it up, milking it for every last drop.

I run to the washroom and splash my face with icy water. I'll tell him I didn't see. I know he didn't notice me there in that crowd, with all those smiling faces. No. My face is blurred beyond the running water, fragile and iridescent. I scrub at the mirror with the back of my hand.

'Hi there,' I say into the mirror. 'Weren't you Somebody once?' And I know I'll laugh a while down the road, because I am still somebody, if only I can remember who.

ANNE CALDWELL

Night out in Bradford

Bellies full of Guinness,
well past closing time, we leave
the warmth of the Beehive pub
link arms and stride out across Lumb Lane.

'Got any cigs?
Where've yer been, out boozin?'
A rag-taggle gang of ten-year-olds
swarms round our skirts.

Drizzle seeps down my jacket collar.
It's a Jack-the-Ripper gloomy night.
Suddenly we're aware of our
lipsticked mouths, high-heeled shoes.

A chrome caravan looms
out of the mist.
Something begins to bark
as we turn down Factory Street.

Teeth are bared. We're cornered.
A rusty chain dangles from its neck;
it's as fucking big as
the Hound of the Baskervilles.

It can smell fear.
I remember the smell of
pee trickling down my leg
outside the headmistress's office.

We inch past.
Teeth sink into my calf.
We're on the run now,
cutting through the park,

two druggies scream
'Piss off you tarts'
My heart's as tight as a fist,
you have your front-door key out ready.

'Bloody stupid walking home!'
your husband shouts,
but we always have,
we were born and bred here.

Two sisters, Monk's Dale, Derbyshire

Out here on the tops
wind snatches our words
flocks of starlings chatter.
The limestone escarpments are grazed knees
in the hillside.

We scramble into Monk's Dale
splattered with mud from the cart track.
Down here the air is green.
We are swimming, hardly breathing.
Our mouths open

then close over years of
borrowing each other's clothes without
asking
fighting over the TV, who got to take the car.
Where can we start?
We don't have a guidebook for the past.

It is fish-tank quiet.
Moss covers boulders.
Lichen drips from silver birch and alder.
The River Dove is serpentine,
clogged with reed-beds like women's hair.

I look for the *Dawn Treader* in the water,
I need a little ship to send you a message.
My glasses are spotted with drizzle.
As usual, you have walked on ahead,
boot-marks one size bigger than mine.

In the forest

An anvil cloud,
like purple soot, masses
above the slate.

Overhead, a swish
of ravens' wings
as they speed towards the quarry.

Wind moans like a beast
trapped in the tubes
of the metal gate.

I turn back from the summit,
pine-needle rain
driving into my cheeks.

Spruce creak
and sigh, the valley air
is thick with resin.

My red wool cloak
is soaked, my basket of bread
feels heavier

and heavier.
I hitch up my skirts.
I mustn't stop.

Your breath is rank, your eyes, amber-coloured slits
your long, stained teeth are grinning.

Flight

She is a gyroscope, thrumming
on the centre of a taut string
held between your fingers.

She is a hot-air balloon
tethered in a parched field.
One blast of fire,
brightly coloured silk
will leave you grounded.

JULIE MELLOR

A *kitten called* Ursula

Mummy left when I was eight years old. She took my baby brother with her and the house was very quiet. I didn't like it because it frightened me. But after that my father found a kitten abandoned in an empty skip at work, and he brought it home. It mewed like an infant.

'What shall I feed it?' I asked him.

'Milk,' he said.

So I held the kitten to me like I had seen Mummy do with the baby, imagining I had boobies. My father said: 'Don't do that, it's dirty.' So I gave the kitten a saucer of milk.

When the kitten had drunk her milk, she crept across the carpet and did a wee in the corner of the room. I had to clean it with washing-up liquid.

I decided to make a house for her out of a cardboard box. I cut a flap for the door and stabbed out four windows with the scissors. No one went in Mummy's room now, so I ripped a large corner off her bedspread and folded it neatly so the kitten would stay warm. My father never said a thing.

The next day, before I went to school, I soaked some cereal in warm milk and spooned it into the kitten's saucer. She lapped it until her tummy was as fat as a balloon, then she staggered around, moving her head from side to side. I thought she was going to be sick. But instead she pawed the carpet, squatted, and did a brown pooh. It had white worms in it. I smacked her like my father had done with me once when I wet my knickers, and flung her into the cardboard box. She cried and snatched at the flap, so I sellotaped it up and took away her saucer.

'Naughty girl,' I said. I didn't feed her for two days.

My father called her 'puss' all the time and soon she started to scamper towards him when he came home from work. I hated it when she ran to him, so I decided to give her a name. Every time I fed her, I bent down low and spoke her name, whispering it in her tiny ear. After a few days the kitten hesitated when my father called, and turned to me because I was whispering her name under my breath. I called her Ursula, after Mummy.

At Christmas she sent me some books. Inside one of them she had written, 'Lots of love from Mummy and Ian.' Ian. I didn't like that name. And I knew my father was right when he said my mother had forgotten me, because all the books were too easy. One of them was called *Bertha's Birthday*, and it had a picture of Bertha blowing out six candles on her cake. The story was silly, but I liked the picture; I wanted Ursula to have a birthday too.

I made her a cake out of some bits of meat which the butcher had given my father. There were fatty pieces, like old chewing gum, and raw frilly slices that smelled bad. My father said I should try boiling it, but he wasn't sure how long for. I found a recipe book in the back of the kitchen cupboard; it still had Mummy's floury fingerprints on the cover. I wiped them off with the dish cloth. I cooked the meat with some carrots and when it was cool my father turned it upside down on to a dinner plate. The pieces of meat were dull and rubbery, suspended in thick jelly. I sprinkled it with salt and pepper, as if it were a huge poached egg.

My father said he was going out. I could smell his after-shave in the kitchen when he had gone.

Once I was alone I pretended it was Ursula's party. I held her paw on the handle of the knife and we made a wish together. I wished that we would always be friends. The jelly shivered as I sliced. It had a strong animal smell and Ursula struggled in my arms. As soon as I let her go she leapt on it, taking great bites and gulping it down without chewing, dipping her head as though she were bobbing apples. It made my mouth water.

I cut another slice and sniffed it as Ursula had done. She watched me, cleaning her whiskers at the same time. She was always washing, hiding her claws away secretively and licking her paws. I crouched on the floor, arched my back, and rested my hands on the carpet. It made the blood rush to my head but I didn't care. I began to eat, pressing my face into the meat. Ursula purred and nuzzled into the crook of my neck.

That night my father came home late. He brought someone with him, a woman. I heard them laughing downstairs and I listened as hard as I could until my father said her name: Andrea.

Ursula would sit on the windowsill for hours, gazing into the garden, her tail spiralling like smoke. Sometimes I pulled it to see what she would do, but she wasn't interested in me. She was watching the little birds dancing from branch to branch. She had never chased a bird because I had never allowed her outside. I didn't trust her: she might run away and leave me.

So I scattered breadcrumbs on the lawn and lay in wait for the starlings myself. I hid behind the dustbin, crouching down, ready to pounce. But the birds were too quick and all I pierced with my sharpened fingernails were some fallen leaves. Ursula eyed me from the window.

When Andrea moved in, my father gave me some extra pocket money. I knew straight away what I wanted to buy: a white mouse from the pet shop. I bought it on the way home from school and released it in my bedroom that night.

'Hickory dickory dock. The mouse ran up the clock.' I remember Mummy singing that to me when I was very small, before my brother was born. But it was just a stupid nursery rhyme. My mouse did not climb up anything. Instead it scuttled under my desk and Ursula didn't know what to do. She was so lazy from being kept indoors that I thought I was going to have to catch it myself.

I lay low on the floor and stared at the mouse without blinking. Ursula did the same. I tucked my neck into my body and curved my back. Ursula copied me. She was such a cheat. I was a much better cat than her. I dug my fingers into the carpet. Then, when I wasn't expecting it, Ursula dived. She did it on purpose, trying to steal my mouse. But it scurried under the bed and would not come out.

Then Ursula grew tired and nearly gave up, so I lifted the corner of the bed to help her a little. She pounced, trapping the mouse between her claws. She would never have done it without me.

Andrea was downstairs. She shouted, 'What's going on up there?'

'Nothing,' I said.

'Get on with your homework or I'll tell your dad.'

The mouse wriggled for a while. It was still alive when Ursula began to eat it. She nibbled her way daintily into its neck and then used her paw to scoop out its brain like a black grape. After that she left the body and went to the windowsill to lick herself. But I knew all that cleaning was just pretend. She covered the same patch of fur again and again. She wasn't doing it to be clean: she was showing off. She preened like a bird and admired her reflection in the glass. It reminded me of the way Andrea licked her finger to smooth her eyebrows. I don't know why Ursula was so proud of herself. I had done most of the work.

Now and then, Ursula returned to the mouse and prowled around it. But she did not eat it until late at night. I stayed up specially to watch.

Mummy had always shopped on the High Street, but Andrea went to the supermarket. She bought pork chops sealed in plastic packs, and rice, and she made everything with salad. My father ate it, even though I knew he liked mashed potatoes and gravy. Andrea bought frozen chickens and we had them roast on Sundays. One teatime I watched my father strip the meat off the bone. The carcass looked like a miniature ship, a brown hull with papery membranes covering secret cavities. My father held out the wishbone, greasy with chicken fat, and offered to pull it with me. But I did not want to snap it in two. I liked it as it was. I wanted to keep it and start a collection.

From that day I saved every wishbone. I gnawed the ends and licked the bones clean behind the locked door of the bathroom. When Ursula ate the mouse she had left the bones in a messy pile. I would do things properly. I lined the drawer of my mother's dressing-table with brown paper and set the wishbones out in order of their size, smallest first. They looked like exhibits in a museum. I padded them underneath with cotton wool, and used my Petite typewriter to make their labels. I knew Ursula was jealous, because she sulked and stared out of the window.

Everything was all right until Andrea bought a new cookery book, full of spicy recipes from foreign countries. She made a chicken korma. It smelled sweet and sickly and had a swirl of yoghurt floating on the top, curdling round the edges. It was worse than school dinners.

I wouldn't eat it. My father said she had spent all day on it. How did I know I didn't like it if I wouldn't even try? He held a piece down to the floor for Ursula and she gobbled it up. 'See, the cat loves it,' he said.

I said: 'I only like roast chicken.'

My father became angry. He started to shout and he banged the table hard, just like he did before Mummy left. Andrea nodded to everything he said, while Ursula padded round his legs and smooched up against him. He said: 'I don't care if you stay there all night. You can have it for breakfast.'

I wanted to spit at him and scratch his eyes out.

He said: 'Don't look at me like that, young lady'. Then he took Andrea out to the pub.

When they had gone, I left the table and went to Mummy's room. I opened the dressing-table drawer and examined my collection. The wishbones were arranged in neat rows, all different sizes, pale and clean as the skin on the inside of my arm. I wished Mummy was there to see them. I opened her wardrobe. She had left some of her clothes behind. There was a red satin dress with bat-wing sleeves. I tried it on. Then I went to the bathroom and smeared Andrea's lipstick around my mouth. I didn't care that it was smudged. I was a real cat, not pretending like Ursula,

When I went downstairs, Ursula was on the table, eating from my plate, licking the thick sauce which had settled around the rim. I could have let her finish, to get rid of it all. But seeing her eat Andrea's food made me angry, so I shooed her away. She sauntered across the room and curled up on my father's chair. Her middle was fat and round and there was a slick of sauce on her whiskers. She had forgotten to wipe her face.

Wait until you're sleeping, I thought. I'll clean you up. I'll pull your dirty whiskers out one by one.

I took the plate, opened the back door, and scraped the sticky remains of the korma into the dustbin, covering it carefully with newspaper and rubbish and pushing it down. My father would never find it.

As I put the lid back I saw Ursula watching me from the kitchen windowsill. But something was wrong. She was on the outside.

I knew I had to move very slowly. I called to her and held out my hand, but she did not come. So I crept up to her, stalking her as if she was a mouse. She drew back and stretched. She was waiting for me to make my next move. I stood quite still for a moment, to confuse her, then I ran towards her as fast as I could, my sharp fingers ready to grab her by the scruff of the neck. But she was too quick, and with a deft spring forward, she melted into the night. I had taught her too well.

I called out to her and even put a saucer of milk outside, but she did not return.

Inside the house it was very quiet. I climbed on to the windowsill and looked out, straining my eyes to see. But nothing moved. I felt hungry because I hadn't eaten my dinner, so I brought Ursula's saucer in and put it on the floor. I knelt down, Mummy's red dress trailing around me, and lapped at the milk until it was all gone. Then I purred in the darkness and curled up under the table where no one would find me.

ANN ATKINSON

Reconstruction

Saturday p.m. 2.44
She checks her watch against the church clock,
sets off through the graveyard. There are
snowdrops, crocuses. There are excavations.
She stops to look into the trench, sees no remains.

The church clock chimes the quarter hour, rooks
make the sound of village, and a dog barks somewhere.

2.54
She takes the path between the bungalows and stables.
A man is digging his garden. She passes two walkers,
says hello. She looks into the stable exercise yard.

It's quiet here, the industry is horses, racing.
The place is full of small people lugging tack.

3.01
Crosses the road, is heading for the stile into the river walk.

Ten, maybe more horses and riders pass. The riders chat
over their shoulders, ride their mounts easy as bikes.
The sound of the shod hooves is like water over stones.

3.10
Note what she is wearing. Reeboks, track-suit, green.
A woman in her forties. She stops by the river.
Watches nothing in particular, lights a cigarette.

The river seems still. She wonders how it calmed
so soon out of the limestone hills. It has cut
the soft earth into sharp banks. Gravel glistens.
There is no obvious water life, no green. The surface
holds it tight like oil, and the sun blinks slowly.

3.24
She walks as far as the next stile. There are two men
talking, one with a rifle cocked over his arm.
She is warm, though the season's early. She turns back.

She is warm, the track-suit's new and green. The sun
clanks off the strange water, so her head is down,
she is looking only at the ground.

The coincidence of sky

All day we watched the sycamore's
dismemberment. The men climbed

like boys with a plan. Balancing
out on a limb, with single-handed

chain-saws, they cut
the ground from underneath their feet.

And all day more and more sky
slid into the space the tree

was leaving. The tree grew taller
with each amputation (its hydraulics

rattled with airlocks) till it was stark
and high as an osprey's roost, and smoke

from the kindling pile rose.
On the same day, she had flown

to the coast, and phoned to say,
look up at the sky at five, and wave.

At five we listened for a small engine
above the snarl of chain-saws, scanned

the sky till it came, pin-silver,
over the valley trees and closer,

dipping over the pitch of the roof.
Look mother. Look grandmother. Look,

I'm flying. We waved from the garden,
dancing, the dog leaping, barking.

And as she circled, we followed, spun
round to the tree as the loudest sound

was a splintering rage and a groan
as the sycamore fell, and the plane

flew through the space where it had been.
She filmed us from the plane.

There's a small blue figure dancing,
an old woman watching, a drift of smoke.

Delicacy

There was a fat moth in the left –
over *Vegetables à la Grecque*, stained
russet in the tomato sauce. A chance

landing while the dish had cooled might
have bogged its legs in. These legs
were up, stiff, all six, pale gold

and cooked. We'd dined by candlelight.
I don't know how I'd not dished up
the sticky corpse onto his plate.

Years ago, by the BBC's light flicker
my father, eating supper (crackers, pickle,
cheese) bit into a moth and retched

loudly, coughing food and moth and both
sets of teeth into his hands, dashed out
to vomit in the kitchen sink. Afterwards

the programme we were watching lost
its thread, him raking up at intervals and
spitting sizzling gobs into the fire.

Moths dive at me as though my face
were lit. I can't rest till they're caught,
shudder at dust on my palms, the hook

of their feet. I did not tell the guest
about the one he'd missed. The chance
moth in the mouth. The indelicacy.

Passing

In a strange town there is a window,
a light through draped curtains, flowers,
a mirror on the wall, a door into the room
opening, as you pass by on a train.

In a strange town inhabit for a short time
a room in which you touch the wax of old wood,
someone's years of touching. Learn quickly
the peculiarities of plumbing, the view out.

What small grief is it, leaving for the last time,
to leave your brief inhabitance alone there
in those moments waiting for the taxi, already
on the other side of the familiar window.

There are perfections of music, passages
you could live in were music not time-bound,
but as it is, passages you might die in.
In love, cheap lyrics (I could die here

in your arms) have shocked, yet there is
no other place beyond that held grace, when
all else is falling back. Spring can't be held.
The sighting of a rare bird is only that.

Time rushes past so fast it leaves you
breathless, and the view is always backwards.
As on a train, back to the engine, eyes
sliding and sliding past strange windows.

The secret of finding lost things

Sunday, 26 January

They want me to write everything down so they can use it in their research. There may be other people like me. 'Jennifer, I want you to leave nothing out,' Dr Murray said. She said this twice, as though she knew I might be tempted.

Of course I'm going to leave certain things out of what I write for *her*. I'm going to write it all here (for you) and write another version for her. Why should I tell her everything? How would it help me?

She's investigating me because I can find lost things. I know that sounds dull, but bear with me. I can find lost objects. Not people – unless a baby or ancient relative has been left behind carelessly in, say, a car park or supermarket. The objects I find would haunt the loser for ever.

Do you remember all that publicity when I found the lottery

ticket for that woman who was going out of her mind about losing it? Did you read how I proved I was genuine by not accepting one single penny of her ten million? (Not in public anyway. What they didn't know was that I'd already accepted a sizeable sum to look in the first place. I have to earn my living like everyone else.) That was when certain people began to see me as a possible stage act, in the category of hypnotists and spoon-benders: theatrical agents heaped offers on me.

But I'm not an entertainer. Mine is a profession. I accept only private clients and for an agreed fee. Recently though, admittedly, I have worked with two NHS referrals. And with the referring GP himself.

These are the objects I have found in the last month: the GP's antique fountain pen; two rings; six earrings; two lockets; a letter (of a most incriminating nature, I might add), five precious teddy bears; Dr Murray's appointment book.

I can't write any more today. Dr Murray (and you) will have to wait.

Monday, 27 January

Will you look at this! Dr Murray has actually written out two questions for me to answer today. (Notice how she uses my name, even when she writes things down. Why do you think she does this?)

Tell me, Jennifer,

 1. *How do you find the objects?*

Answer: I watch the loser. Then I recreate that division of mind and body when our thoughts are in one place and our hand is in another. Or when we aren't alert to the tinkling falling of an earring, or the breeze which displaces a letter. (This isn't all. But I certainly don't intend to write this next bit in Dr Murray's version. You see, I know whether the object wants to be returned or not. Lost objects have an ambivalence: sometimes they're angry. On the other hand, I'll always return a child's toy.)

2. *Why have you got this power, Jennifer?*

Answer: I myself am lost. My parents lost me. Over time, they misplaced their instinct for loving me. I loved a man once, but he frequently forgot I was there beside him, and acted as though he was alone. People lose my telephone number, forget an essential part of my address. (You can skip the rest of this answer, if you like. It tells Dr Murray all she wants to know, but she won't see it.) You'll have noticed that I can't shut my eyes. I never sleep. I see everything. I've spent my life observing the electricity of loss: little moments of change so unbearable that most of us blink to avoid them. When I was eleven, I waited in the grass for two days and three nights by the last harebell, watching for the exact moment when the winter wind whipped its petals away for ever. And when that tiny scrap of blue sur-rendered, I went with it on a journey far beyond the existence of angels. I left my body below, staring at the stars: another small hurdle for the wind. (I *told* you – my parents lost me. They remembered if I reminded them – and of course that was nec-essary sometimes. After the loss of the harebell, for example, I was quite ill with exposure.)

A further note of explanation: I'm easy to lose. I'm thin and I'm dark like a shadow. And no one puts any effort into finding a girl who can't shut her eyes. (But I'm *beautiful* – especially when I'm found, and I'm as full of longing and anger as any-thing else that's lost.)

Tuesday, 28 January

Today, Dr Murray has asked for case studies, examples of how I found a lost thing. Why doesn't she ever ask what the lost things tell me?

This is the case study she really wants. It's for you. I'm not going to give it to her. I may tantalise her with its existence later on.

The client was Lora (*sic*) Candale. What's left to say about this woman? You'll know that she's here, in London, to make a low-budget, supposedly prestigious British film to redeem her last Hollywood failure. You'll have read about her beauty, her incredible figure (a bounty given to anyone who can photograph the tiniest bit of cellulite on her body – and remember Lora herself offered the bounty). Probably, having seen some of her films (what did you think of *Four Steps after Midnight*?), you'll have formed your own opinion as to her talent. No doubt you've been gripped, and later bored, by her three marriages and three divorces with the same man. You'll have concluded that this latest reconciliation, and even the much-publicised loss of the utterly priceless engagement ring, is a stunt to revive her career (and gain sympathy) after that film.

'No it's not a fucking publicity stunt,' she hissed at me when I asked. (I was playing with her. I knew that her ring was lost.) 'Can you find it or can't you?'

'I can find it.'

I looked around the hotel room – the bridal suite – for somewhere to sit. The bed and sofas were covered in ice-cream satin. The chairs were ormolu-encrusted and laughably fragile. I remained standing. 'Talk to me about your ring.'

'Talk to you about my ring?' Lora stared at me, ran a hand

through that orange hair, and hissed at me again: 'You've got the insurance photo.'

'I need to hear you talk about the ring,' I insisted. 'When do you last remember touching it?'

For a second, she pressed her eyes shut. (How I ached with envy at those tightly shut eyes.) Then she indicated the whole room: 'Last Wednesday. Here. I was right here.'

'Alone?'

'Uh huh.' (Interesting how this can be said evasively.)

'And the room's obviously been cleaned since then?'

'Yeah, and the dust-bag taken apart every goddamn day. What else do you need to know? You will find it?'

I was tired of this charade. I knew where to find the ring. 'I need to be alone,' I said. Lora picked up one of her pink telephones and called for her car.

Alone, I sat on the ice-cream satin sofa and stretched out my hand to a pot which held an obscure cactus. I dug deeply into the sand and touched a certain portion of the stem. It opened easily, like a door. I drew out the ring and lifted it to my lips. I blew the sand from the setting and placed in my palm the 41.37 carat flawless stone: the Medici diamond.

Later, I left a note for Lora saying that I'd failed to find her ring and suggested the reason for this was that it had been not lost, but stolen.

Yes, yes. I lied. What does that matter?

29 January. Recorded message from Dr Murray
(CONFIDENTIAL)

I need to hurry this up. Jennifer is taking forever to tell this story. The police found absolutely no evidence of theft whatsoever, but in

*the course of the investigation, Lora mentioned that she felt uneasy
about Jennifer. Those staring eyes. Drugs? The police decided to
investigate. In Jennifer's house they found not only Lora's ring,
but an Aladdin's cave of baubles: probably all stolen. Furthermore,
I know that Jennifer is writing two versions. Most of our clients do.
It gives them a feeling of power. Our approach is designed to
encourage it. I know everything that Jennifer has told you. There's
nowhere to hide a second account in her cell. Jennifer will be
released in six days and I'm preparing an important research
paper on her. You realise that Jennifer is cunning, an absolute
master of carefully planned spontaneity? But the fact is that she
does have an extraordinary ability to locate lost objects and I'm no
nearer to understanding how she does this. We believe she is about
to explain herself to you. You are our most trusted prison visitor
and I'm not asking you to break confidentiality. However, I'd be
grateful if you would come to see me when you have seen Jennifer.*

Thursday, 30 January

She's told you. I could see from your expression. I haven't lost
you completely, have I? You know I'm telling you the truth,
don't you? Here, I'll tell you what Lora Candale's ring told me.

Anger! Lora's tantrums were endlessly humiliating. She once
threw the Medici diamond down the lavatory; twice hurled it
into the garden; once under a car. She hid it whenever her latest
lover appeared (that's why she pulled off the ring and ground it
into the cactus, somehow getting it mixed up with stubbing
out her cigarette). Lora actually used the Medici diamond as a
weapon. She turned the ring round into her palm and slashed
her then husband across the cheek, slicing it to the bone. The
Medici diamond has no wish to be found by its owner.

Yes. I admit my possession of this ring might seem suspicious, but look at the rest of what Dr Murray calls baubles. Who would steal a broken marcasite bracelet with two of the charms missing? Who would steal a little china Bambi? You'd regard these things as trash, throwaway stuff. Do you realise there's a layer of the earth's crust reserved for lost things? Sometimes, in the darkness, they lose their anger, change their minds and beg to be found. Archaeology is a wonderful vocation. I may take it up myself.

I can't help them in this cell. These walls muffle their stories. How can I play my piano to them? They always ask for Chopin when the north wind blows. I must sing to them. There's a special love song for lost things. It reminds them of when they mattered. They need their love songs on a frosty night.

Dr Murray still doesn't understand how I find lost things. She believes it's an illusion, a confidence trick. The poor woman can bear only her own reality. Surely this is the very converse of scientific objectivity? I know you agree. Last week when you asked me to find your diary, you said, 'I'm sure it's staring me in the face and laughing'. And it was. (By the way, your diary has no ambivalence about being found. It finds your forgetfulness amusing.)

I suspect you already know the truth. Which is this: I have never in my whole life stolen or found an object which was lost. These things come to me to make me beautiful and I go to them to make them loved again. All these trinkets, all these once-significant, once-beloved things. They found me.

EILEEN MOELLER

Sunny like a tree

breaks the blue horizon
stuck in the red dirt of this place
and reaching up to heaven
with pleading limbs.

Well, not really.
She'd never get anywhere doing that
what with the bag dragging at her waist
that won't go filling itself.

But once in a while she looks up
and that big old leafless thing
seems to be on fire:
calling through God's thin ether,
telling Him: *See, look here,*
this isn't how you made us.
This isn't right at all.

Eileen Moeller

Sunny tough hands

from pulling that soft white stuff
out of the claws that hold it tight.

No softness, nothing white without a price..
Her Mama has told her that in how many ways?

Soon as she had ears to hear and eyes to see.

Sunny too fat

made her brothers laugh,
said her butt jiggled and quivered
like the skin that held the river in.

Right, she said.
And if you don't stop pinchin' and brushin' past me
I'll throw myself in there and wash away for good.

Ssss, Sunny, come on, sit down with me.
Mama putting the plates out,
just the two of them, for biscuits and honey
and hot sweet camomile tea.

Mama always fixin' it,
the miserable din of her brothers, the dogs, the fields
all receding in the hum of pleasure,
the two of them drunk like bees.

Eileen Moeller

Sunny in the cotton field

looking distant as she bends
to rest the heavy sack on the ground.

Why's Sunny so dreamy today?
Her look so far away:
probably back at the house
where her baby cries
and nobody's pickin' it up.

Sunny's big arms ache.
Her breasts gone dry
so the baby can feed
while she's away.

What is that girl thinkin' of?
Sitting out on the porch,
dozing off when she should be inside.

Sunny hates being tied to this
heavy weight thing
when her baby is light as a feather
and all that sweet going to waste on a little girl
who no time ago was playing with dolls.

Sunny strokes the back of her own hand for comfort
and leans into her work.

Sunny dark chocolate

Sweet, uh-huh. That's what she says to herself
when the little white girl on the bus

points a finger pale as a maggot at her,
says *Look, Mama. Look.*
A lady like a candy bar.

Then the bus goes shameful and silent just for a heartbeat,
but it's enough to give Sunny an ache in her neck
from holding her head up
as she lowers herself out the back door.

During his lectures
he notices

that her back is a straight garden wall
from which the breasts
cascade like clusters of heavy blossoms.

He imagines God's head resting there
on the startling blue of her dress,
God's hand that sweats
and wrinkles what covers her thighs.

His eyes follow her pencil.
How lightly she holds it, how she resists
putting his grey interpretations across
the white expanse of her notebook.

White. White moons in her nails. White sliding
down a sheer stockinged leg.
Her shoe like a narrow black canoe with a bow:
he will take her
across the lake of his desire some day soon.

He will begin to plead with her on paper:
Without you, he will write,
I am the soul of a rat, a crimson abnegation.
Without you – nothing but a hammer
striking the Pietà, shit
on the head of the Buddha.

Vincent loves Lucy

It would've gone this way:
him taking her to his little room at Arles
after ditching Ricky in Paris,
the Cuban left scratching his head at the station,
trying to figure out which train his dizzy wife had boarded by
                                                            mistake.

It would start out like a dream,
guileless as the gleaners in the fields:
her speaking her cartoon French to make him laugh;
him whispering that her rosebud mouth
was the keyhole that would release them both.

But it wouldn't take long for him to start throwing the knives,
for the two of them to reach combustion you might say,
what with all that flaming improbable hair.

Picture the scenes:
the two of them so fair and sailing over wheat-grass,
the lift of her parasol, him coaxing her up into the wind,
on to the delicate scaffolding of the Langlois drawbridge.

Then all of a sudden her skirt gets caught,
the stubborn tilt of her hat as she yanks and yanks,
the boats crowding in unable to get through
and Vincent making no move to help,
only trying to paint her refusal,
only blotting out her reflection with thick black strokes.

Of course she'd spill unwanted into his work then:
the orange doorways, the frantic slashes of sunlight, the crows
singing badly in the fields.

These brushes with immortality aren't made to last.
The whole thing, for Lucy, too much
like being locked inside of a steamer trunk,
for Vincent, a mouth overfull of chocolates.

Before you know it there's a telegram waiting for Ricky at the
                                                    hotel desk.
Help, it says. *I tried to buy a painting but the guy misunderstood me.*
Can you and Fred and Ethel pick me up?

ALISON DUNNE

Buying a gun

I told Della about the gun.

 'You'd be better off with a dishwasher,' she said.

Since he died I've dreamed about buying a gun.

I looked at dishwashers in the Electricity Showroom.

 'They're so easy, so convenient,' the sales assistant said.
With their soft-opening stay-where-you-put-them doors; the
inner racks on soundless rollers.

 'They're quiet,' the sales assistant said. 'And they'll wash
your dishes beautifully while you're asleep. Because there is
this button –' the sales assistant pointed to the button. With a
flourish. Like she'd invented it.

Since he died, I've been killing myself. Driving fast without a
seat-belt. Smoking. Drinking gin.

*

'I can't afford a dishwasher,' I said. 'I'm saving for a gun.' And I patted my hip where I'd hang a pouch of gunpowder.

'Well,' said the assistant. Rubbing palms together. Eyes leaking off to where a couple were considering fridges.

'I've no need for a dishwasher now,' I tell Della. 'The amount of dishes I make.' On my own.

Della is on her exercise bike. 'I imagine I'm cycling somewhere,' she says.

'Where, Della?'

'Oh, anywhere. It's usually hills. Green fields. The country, you know.'

I know the country. Wasn't I brought up there? In the country. In the village. Didn't I ride the lanes on a real bike? Ride really? It was the only way to get anywhere. Haven't I wriggled into the earth, into underground dens?

'I know the country,' I tell Della. And Della says, 'I know you do.' She's doing a counselling course at the University Centre. She's always telling me about her modules.

His death had been sudden. Unexpected. Premature.

Della is still cycling. She is filmed with sweat. 'You should go on a course. What do you fancy? There are some that are not too taxing.' Next term she's doing a new module: Bereavement Counselling.

'It's a pity you didn't do it last term,' I tell her.

'Never mind,' says Della. 'You'll still be grieving. I can catch up with you.'

I decided to buy a gun, but didn't know how to go about it. No *Which?* guide. No *Which Weapon?*

*

'I've been reading for Bereavement next term,' Della says. I'm sure she has. Della is a good student. I've seen her through the patio door, cycling to nowhere, a book balanced on the handlebars.

'There are distinct phases,' she says. 'I can't remember them all, in order, but I think there's denial and anger.'

What about relief?

'I can't remember the other one. Guilt, maybe.'

It's a good guess, guilt. It could come into anything. And does. But denial is more interesting.

'I've just read an article on denial,' I tell Della.

'Ooh,' says Della, wiping her upper lip with her wrist sweat-band. It surprises Della that I read anything. Oh you'd be surprised, Della. You'd say 'Ooh'.

'Yes,' I say. 'The thirteenth-century etymological root is "saying no to".'

'So you're saying no to a death?' Della is thinking. And I'm thinking: Not that it does you any good. 'No. I don't want my mother/father/partner/child (delete where applicable) to die.' It would be disastrous for the insurance business.

Della's Peter is in insurance. 'A mere claims clerk,' he says, but with a glitter to his eyeballs that makes my skin caterpillar up and down me. He's a man with delusions. Thinks he's really a spy or double agent; that each fire-damaged curtain or stolen bike is code for International Skulduggery.

'If I owned a gun, Peter,' I asked him once, 'would my premiums go up?' But Peter didn't know.

'I shouldn't think so,' he blustered. 'Anyway, how would they know? It isn't exactly on the form next to smoking, height and weight.'

'How can they tell you're a smoker?' I asked. 'Do they sniff your application form? What if it had last been handled by a postal worker recently back from a fag break in the yard?'

Peter looked uncomfortable. 'Do you own a gun?' he asked.

'I'm saving up for one,' I told him, and Peter invented a job in the shed that simply had to be done.

Della is still cycling. 'I'm heading for the city now,' she says. 'Sheffield,' she says. 'I need something arduous. Sheffield's hard going as cities go.'

'Built on seven hills. Like Rome,' I tell her.

'I'd be better off in Norwich,' Della says, breathing hard.

Sheffield: where I might have gone to college if I'd got the grades. I don't tell Della that. 'For a city,' I tell Della, 'it's very green. The most parks per capita in Europe.'

'Really?' says Della. People are often surprised.

'And a dry ski slope,' I tell her. 'Though dry is a misnomer, Della,' I say.

He was such a fit man. So young. His eating moderate, his drinking recreational. He always drove with care. No mad overtaking.

Della is slowing, puffing.

'Where to now?'

'I'm in Holland,' she says. 'I go to Holland when I get knackered. It's good and flat.' Della doesn't have an adjusting knob that makes pedalling harder, easier, middling. She changes it in her head.

'Are you calling in at Amsterdam?'

'No,' she says. 'It's all bridges and hash cafés and red-light districts,' she says.

*

I was going to Amsterdam once. With him. Before he died. I didn't want to. I don't like to travel. I'm lazy, would rather stay at home with comforts and not have to unpack. I couldn't decide what he wanted to go for.

'You can hire a bike for fourteen guilders a day,' he'd said. I wouldn't have touched drugs. Then. Walking through red-light districts would have upset me. And I think: So much I've wanted a gun; wanted to load it like a musket, tamp it down. To shoot.

'They have women in shop windows, naked,' I tell Della. 'Displayed like fruit. To buy.'

'Oh I know,' she says. 'Peter went there on a stag weekend, once. Of course he had to go round with the others, although he didn't like it.'

Much. I am thinking of his glittery deluded-spy eyeballs zigzagging across the shop fronts.

Then I have an image of thin red metal folded into mountains and valleys, concertinaed, shearing. Smoke running up into the air and petrol, like gin, hurrying across tarmac.

'I've decided not to buy a gun,' I say to Della.

'Really?' says Della.

'Yes. I'd like to do a course.'

'Really?' says Della. The cycling stops.

'I'll start with something that's not too taxing.'

'I know just the thing,' says Della. 'Just the thing.'

SALLY BAKER

Fake leopard-skin coat

Where I come from the word is *Tart*
mouthed in the same breath as
What does she think she looks like?
but I love the feel of it, slipped
over shoulders over satin; long
for red lipstick and platinum, hoops
for my ears. I cannot resist.

In the café a woman is helped
to her chair and brought tea.
Windows steam. A mother and daughter
in matching track-suits smoke
by the door. The same life lived over twice.
My coat sidles on the chair back, proud,
where I can feel it, spot side out.

At the bus stop a woman in green
has done up her hair in tights, her cheeks
rouged a fierce red. She sings.
I blow her a kiss, dreaming of sixty
and outfits to come; the courage of colour,
of shining out from the ordinary.
What does she think she looks like?

All day I have it near me, my coat,
laid in my lap in the car,
subdued and sleepy, stroking the fur
and folding my hands in the sleeve.
Something of me survived the journey
away and back through years. The words
I *am home* on my lips, wherever that is.

Where flooding
is possible

Flood warning is not an exact science.
Flood warnings are colour-coded like traffic lights.
Even sea walls and river banks can be breached
during extreme rainfall or rough seas.
Block doorways and airbricks with sandbags.
Move livestock and tractors to higher ground.
Bring the chickens indoors.
Move to an upper floor with irreplaceable items
such as photographs, old letters and antique silk dresses.
Wear your grandmother's garnet ring.
Take warm clothes, food, a torch, people and pets.
A battery-powered radio may be useful.
Don't take overdue library books or red bills.
Don't stop to answer the telephone
or take your pie out of the microwave.
Take the piece of amber you found on the beach.
Leave the grandfather clock facing out to sea.
Leave the front door open.

Biographical notes

LIZ ATKIN was born in Lincolnshire in 1951 and now lives in Newcastle upon Tyne. She trained as a visual artist at St Martin's School of Art in London, going on to have exhibitions in the UK and Europe. Three years ago she gave up drawing for a long-held desire to write poetry and has since had work published in many poetry magazines.

ANN ATKINSON was born in 1947 and lives in the Peak District. She has taught creative writing at Derby University and Bretton Hall and now teaches for the Workers' Education Association and Sheffield University Division of Continuing Education. She completed an MA in Contemporary Poetry at Manchester University in 1994 and was a prize-winner in both the York and Cardiff poetry competitions in 1997.

SALLY BAKER was born in Suffolk in 1961 and now lives in Yorkshire. Her poems have won prizes in several competitions including the Ilkley Literature Festival and the *Staple* magazine competition in 1997. 'Fake leopard-skin coat' was broadcast on Radio 3 and shortlisted for the Forward Prize for Best Poem in 1996.

SUZANNE BATTY was born in Devon in 1963, but grew up in Manchester, where she now lives. She performs her work solo and as part of a women's writing group. She is involved in promoting women's writing in Manchester, where she is planning to launch a new literary magazine in 1998.

CARIL BEHR was born in South Africa in 1947, but has spent most of her adult life in the UK. She teaches art to adults with special needs at a further education college in London and the original metal jewellery she makes has been exhibited in the UK and Europe. Although she has been writing for years, she only recently began submitting work for publication. One of her stories won the first *Queer Words* competition in 1996.

JADWIGA BILLEWICZ was born in London in 1948, raised in Aberdeen and now lives in County Durham. She was studying for her doctorate in French Language and Literature when she changed direction completely to design and make jewellery for a living. She has come back to writing consistently in recent years, concentrating on poetry and short stories.

PAM BRIDGEMAN was born in Lancashire in 1950. For the past twenty years she has lived in Cumbria, where she teaches in a sixth-form college for the Open University. Her work has appeared in several magazines and in the *No Holds Barred* anthology (Women's Press, 1985). She gained a Northern Arts writing award in 1997 to work on a collection.

ANNE CALDWELL was born in Surrey in 1964 and is now based in Manchester, working as a Literature Development Officer in Oldham. She studied English and American Literature at the University of East Anglia and has had her poetry published in a variety of magazines.

ALISON DUNNE was born in Lancashire in 1964 and now lives in Leicestershire. After a spell as a performance poet, she now works full-time as a Literature Development Officer for Leicestershire, and part-time as a creative-writing tutor in adult education. Her stories have won competitions and have been broadcast on BBC Radio 4.

STEPHANIE HALE was born in 1966 and lives in Oxford. She trained in print journalism and progressed to working as a news reporter for local and national radio and television. She studied creative writing at the University of East Anglia then became Literature Development Officer for Buckinghamshire. She now writes full time.

HARRIET KLINE was born in Devon in 1971. After studying English and Drama at Bristol, she worked as a volunteer at a women's centre and with women's writing groups in York. She is currently Writer in Residence for a hospital arts organisation in the Isle of Wight, where she also runs a writing group.

LINDA LEATHERBARROW was born in Scotland in 1946 and now lives in London, where she works as a tutor in creative writing and is co-organiser of the Haringey Literature Festival. She is three times first prize-winner of the London Writers' Competition and her stories have been published in magazines, in the *Sleeping Rough* anthology (Lime Tree, 1991) and broadcast on BBC Radio 4.

CLAIRE LYNN was born in 1965. She taught English in a teacher-training college in China from 1988 to 1990. She now lives in Northumberland and works as an itinerant part-time tutor in the west of Newcastle, teaching adults on access courses.

LISA MATTHEWS was born in Newcastle upon Tyne in 1967 and works at the City Library as a designer in the Art Department. She is co-founder and organiser of the Blue Room, a woman-only performance space in Newcastle. She is currently studying for an MA in Creative Writing at Northumbria University.

JULIE MELLOR was born in Sheffield in 1966. She has lived in Spain and Italy and done a variety of jobs, from au pair work to sales and marketing. She graduated from the University of Huddersfield in 1996 and is currently studying for an MA in Creative Writing at Sheffield Hallam.

EILEEN MOELLER is an American born in 1950, who has lived and worked in the UK since 1995. She has an MA in Creative Writing from Syracuse University and has been published in a number of US journals and two women's anthologies published by Beacon Press. While living in London she was a member of the writing group Women and Words based at the Riverside Studios.

CANDY NEUBERT lives in Devon. She recently spent six years in South Africa, which has greatly influenced her writing. Her poetry is widely published in South Africa and one of her stories was shortlisted for the Ian St James Award for short fiction.

WENDY RICHMOND was born in 1953 and lives in Sheffield, where she teaches creative writing and works as an editor and script editor. She also paints and is incorporating this increasingly into her poetry. She enjoys working with actors, employing acting techniques for devising and discovering in her work.

ANNE SUMMERFIELD was born in 1958 and lives in Hampshire. After years as a technical writer in the computer industry, she escaped to do an MA in the Theory and Practice of Modern Fiction and is now working on a PhD on women's short stories. Her story, 'The velvet maid', won an Asham Award in 1996, was published in *The Catch* anthology (Serpent's Tail, 1997) and broadcast on BBC Radio 4.

GERALDINE TAYLOR was born in Kent in 1946 and now lives in Bristol, where she is Educational Consultant to Ladybird Books, works as a counsellor and co-runs the First Paragraph writing group for women. She is a prolific non-fiction author and her books about wildlife have won many awards. She only recently began writing short stories, but is already winner of several national competitions.

LAUREEN VONNEGUT was born in the US but has been living in Bulgaria for three years. Before becoming a full-time writer, she managed a law firm in California. Her stories have been widely published in the US and are being translated into Bulgarian.

AMANDA WHITE was born in London in 1965, where she works as a literary agent and writes poetry, short and long fiction and edits books. Her prize-winning poetry has appeared in numerous literary magazines.

JULIA WIDDOWS was born in London in 1955 and now lives in Brighton. She has been writing fiction ever since she could use a pen but has only recently submitted her work for publication. Since then she has been successful in the 1996 Ian St James and the 1997 *Stand* magazine competitions and has had work published in *The Catch* anthology (Serpent's Tail, 1997).

JANE WOOD was born in Surrey in 1949 but has lived in Newcastle upon Tyne all her adult life. She started writing seriously six years ago and is currently studying for an MA in Creative Writing at the University of Northumbria. She is co-founder and organiser of the Blue Room, a woman-only performance space in Newcastle.